Shortie Like Mine

Shortie Like Mine

NI-NI SIMONE

KENSINGTON PUBLISHING CORP.
http://www.kensingtonbooks.com

DAFINA BOOKS are published by

Kensington Publishing Corp.
850 Third Avenue
New York, NY 10022

All Kensington titles, imprints, and distributed lines are
available at special quantity discounts for bulk purchases
for sales promotion, premiums, fund-raising, educational,
or institutional use.

Special book excerpts or customized printings can also
be created to fit specific needs. For details, write or phone
the office of the Kensington Special Sales Manager:
Kensington Publishing Corp., 850 Third Avenue, New
York, NY 10022. Attn. Special Sales Department. Phone:
1-800-221-2647.

Dafina Books and the Dafina logo Reg. U.S. Pat. & TM Off.

ISBN-13: 978-0-7582-2839-0
ISBN-10: 0-7582-2839-2

First Printing: August 2008
10   9   8   7

Printed in the United States of America

For Taylor and Sydney, a few years from now . . .
and to my cousin RaShea,
for the day we sat in the mall
and dreamed up Melvin.

Acknowledgments

My Father, Christ Jesus, I thank You for Your multitude of blessings. Your word said all I had to do was ask it in Your name; I did, and here I am. Thank You Lord, for continuing to see beyond my faults and straight to my dreams.

To my mother and father, I love you for all of your support and for always being there for me. I couldn't do any of this without you.

To Kevin, for always being my number one fan!

To Taylor, Sydney, and Zion, I do all of this for you!

To my family, I love each and every one of you, and to my cousins: John, Taniesha, Kaareem, Malik, and Sharief, thanks for all of the childhood memories that I can now sit back and write about.

To Nakea Murray, for knowing from day one that this was possible. To Selena James, for the opportunity, glad we're back together again! To Melody Guy, for being the best. To Mercedes Fernandez, thanks for your assistance with this project. And to all of my author friends for always being there and listening to my stories no matter what, you mean the world to me!

To all of the book stores, book clubs, websites, fans, coworkers, and message boards—thanks a million for your support!

And to all of the lil' mamas who wear their thickness well, I wrote this for you! Be sure to send me a friend request on MySpace at myspace.com/nini_simone or email me at *ninisimone@yahoo.com*, and tell me what you think about *Shortie Like Mine*!

Hollah!

1

I ain't even gonna front . . .
Since you walked up in the club
I've been giving you the eye . . .
Must be a full moon . . .

　　　—BRANDY, "FULL MOON"

It was official: I was fly. I had on my freakum dress and the fat version of Lil Wayne was stalking me. Everywhere I looked, there he was. Grinning. As if somebody here in Newark, New Jersey told him he was cute. He had drips of sweat running from his temples to his chin and was breathing like he was having an asthma attack. I was embarrassed. Out of all the tenders lined up outside the club, hugged up on their honeys, and kicking it with their boys, here I was being harassed by a baby gorilla in a short set.

My girls and I were in line, waiting to get in to Club Arena for teen night, and for the first time in my life, I was appreciating my size fourteen brick-house hips. My hair was done in a cute ponytail, swinging to the side with a swoop bang in the front, my MAC was poppin', and my stilettos were workin' it out.

I resembled a voluptuous New New from *ATL*: two deep dimples, honey glazed skin, full lips, and dark brown eyes shaped like a lost reindeer. My sleeveless House of Dereon dress was the color of new money and the belt wrapped around my waist was metallic silver. My colorful bangles and big hoop earrings were courtesy of Claire's and the rose tattoo on my left calf was by way of the 99 Cent Store and warm water. So, you get the picture? Fierce was written all over me. And just when I started feeling comfortable with being the biggest one in my all-girl clique, tragedy struck . . .

"Yo, Shawtie!" my stalker screamed as if he were working at the Waffle House, making a public service announcement. He was standing at the door talking to one of the bouncers, when my friend Deeyah walked up and stood beside me. "Yo, Shawtie," he called again. "Deeyah"—he raised his arm in the air as if he were making a three-point play—"that's me right there."

My girls and I all looked around. We ain't know who the *heck* he was talking about.

"Seven, there go your new boo." Deeyah blew a pink bubble and popped it. "The one and only Melvin. Told you I was gon' hook you up."

Melvin? I tugged Deeyah on her arm. "Is this a joke?"

"What's wrong with him?" she snapped, rolling her eyes. "You tryna talk about my taste?"

Ni-Ni Simone

Oh . . . my . . . God . . . I'ma die. "He looks like my sixty-year-old Cousin Shake."

"Everything is not about looks, Seven. When are you gon' to grow up and learn that?"

"When I'm done with being sixteen, which is not today. I don't believe this."

"Well, who did you think you were gon' get?" She popped her gum and smiled. "After all, Josiah is mine and the rest of his crew, well . . . I hooked them up," she said as she pointed at each of our friends: Ki-Ki, Yaanah, and Shae.

Ki-Ki and Yaanah shot me a snide grin as if to say, *That's right!* But Shae rolled her eyes and said, "Please, Deeyah. You lucky I ain't punch you in the face for that. Gon' hook me up with somebody named Shamu."

"Shamu is a nice name." Deeyah jerked her neck.

"But he followed me around in school." Shae sighed. "From class to class, and then I come to find out he was the oldest kid in special ed."

"Special ed?" Deeyah pointed to her chest. "He's in my class. So what you tryna say, Shae? So what if he wears a helmet? He needs love, too."

A helmet?

"Why"—Shae looked toward the sky—"do I even go through this?"

"Go through what?" Deeyah smirked. "Why don't you think about the future, Shae? Don't you know people in special ed get a check every month? Never mind, Shae. You just played yourself." She turned her attention back to me. "Seven, I know you got more sense than this chick, so you know you need a man that you gon' complement. Trust me. See Josiah, needs a chick like me. I'm a dime and you're a quarter. Josiah is the captain of the basketball team and Melvin over there"—she pointed—"is the team. Make sense?"

We all looked at Deeyah like she was stupid. "Can you say dumb-dumb?" I shook my head. "You so busy tryna dis me that you actually just gave me and ole boy over there a compliment."

"Girl, please. That flew over your head," Deeyah snapped. "You just played yourself."

"Deeyah, you just said you were a dime and she was a quarter." Shae sighed. "Get a clue."

"I could get a clue if I could stop passing it to you." Deeyah rolled her eyes. "Y'all so stupid. I'm tired of being the mother of this played-out group. Anyway, Seven, I called myself doing you a favor."

"A favor?"

"Yeah, I'm tryna save you from being played."

"Excuse you?!" I could've smacked her.

"Think of it this way. If a guy is too fly, he might leave you for a skinny chick." She ran her hands along the sides of her body. "And with Rick Ross over there"—she snickered—"you ain't got to worry 'bout that."

Before I could decide if I wanted to body her or simply cuss her out, I felt a tap on my shoulder and hot breath on my neck. "What's good, Shawtie?" It was Melvin, looking me up and down as if he

4

could take a biscuit and sop me up with his eyes. "I knew I'd seen you before—good look, Deeyah."

"You've seen me?" *I don't think I've been to hell yet.*

"Yeah, I pass you everyday on my way to English class."

"Really?" I was beyond disgusted.

"Come on, Shawtie, ain't you in them honor's classes? You real smart and er'thang." He had the biggest grin I'd ever seen. "My pot'nahs call me Big Country. But my name is Melvin. I just moved here from Murfreesboro."

"Murphy who?"

"Carolina, Shawtie." His gold tooth was gleaming. "You know, I-95 in the house, the dirty-dirty baby."

I was speechless. Not only was he fat, he was country.

"Speechless, huh? You ain't never seen nobody reppin' for the dirty-dirty like me befo'." As if he had a bullhorn and was doing the lean-back, he cupped each hand on the sides of his mouth and shouted, "MUR . . . FREES . . . BORO!!!"

God must hate me.

"I know you feelin' me, Shawtie." He grabbed me by the arm and pulled me toward him. "Gurl, you so sharp, you hurtin' me. Now, let's get on in here. You ain't got to wait in no line. We just gon' walk on in this piece. Now ya gurls, I can't do nothin' for them. Big Country's pull is limited."

"Oh, it's okay." I shook my head. "Really, it is. I'll just wait with them. You go on."

"Sab, Shawtie." He pinched my cheek. "I was just playin'. Psyched yo' mind." He ran his index finger across my forehead. "Y'all get on here and come on in this piece. Deeyah and Shawtie, y'all hold arms and y'all other two walk in front of me and let them know Big Country has arrived."

"That's all you, Melvin?" someone shouted as we walked in.

"All day playboy," he shouted back. "All day."

Jesus please . . .

As soon as we walked in, the base in the music sent vibrations through the floor. The D.J. was doing his thang—Baby Huey's "Pop, Lock, and Drop It" was playing and instantly, everyone, including Melvin, started dancing. I stood leaning from one foot to the other, wondering what punishment I faced next.

And just when I decided I should find a rock to climb under, Melvin threw his hands in the air and screamed, "This my jam right here!!" "Walk It Out" started playing and Melvin took to the floor again.

After the song finished, Melvin bought me a drink and dragged me to take a few Polaroids with him. In the midst of him squattin', leanin', and showcasin' a few jailhouse poses with me standing completely still, Josiah, Deeyah's boyfriend and number twenty-three on the school's basketball team, swaggered over with an entourage of his teammates. Two things about Josiah and his crew is that they were the finest in school and all the girls wanted them. But me, I only had eyes for Josiah and when I found out Deeyah was dating him, I think I passed out everyday for a week straight. She must've stolen him out of my dreams because that's the only way I could see me allowing her to walk away with him. Other than that, we woulda been throwin'. Please believe dat. But since I didn't think I had a real chance of him liking me, I stepped to the side and have been diggin' him from afar.

Josiah had a super-sized Uptown in his hand. He shook the ice, handed the cup to Deeyah, and she finished it off. Then he stood behind her with his fingers locked around her waist, his chin on top of her head, and he started staring at me.

Chris Brown's "Shortie Like Mine" was playing and for a moment I could swear Josiah's eyes were singing the lyrics to me. This made me want him even more. The crush I had on him was unshakable. He was not only the most wanted man in school, he was the best looking. He was so beautiful I was tempted to call him pretty. He superseded fine and gorgeous couldn't touch him. He was the type of dude that should've been a poster child for irresistible. Most people said he favored the rapper Nelly, but personally, I thought he put Nelly to sleep. He was so fine it didn't make sense. He was at least six feet, with skin the color of caramel in its richest form, the sexiest almond-shaped eyes in the world, and a fresh Caesar with brushed-in waves. His gear was always dapper: baggy jeans, an oversize skull belt buckle, a fitted black tee that read "I am Hip Hop," and throwback Pumas.

8

"Can't speak, Seven?" he asked.

I know he had to hear my heart beating. "No," I snapped, and as an extra twist, I rolled my eyes.

"Yo, Josiah," Melvin interrupted. "Back up off me now. You know this is me right here."

"Yo, my fault son." He smiled. "Do you."

"Whew, Shawtie," Melvin said, dapping sweat like a church lady in heat. "Give ya boo a sip of that soda."

Oh, he had me messed up. There was no way we'd reached the level of drinking after one another. "You see the bar over there." I pointed. "Go fetch yo'self one."

"Fetch?" Josiah snapped. "He ain't a dog."

"Is that why you responded?" I asked.

"You tryna say I'ma dog?"

"I'm tryna say you all up in here wit' it." I waived my hand under my chin as if I were slicing it.

"Dang, Shawtie, you just angry, huh?" Melvin said. "What, you P.M.S.'n or somethin'? Somebody hook my girl up with some Midol."

His girl?

"Now, Shawtie," Melvin went on, "act right in front of company and gimme some of that soda." He snatched the cup from my hand and I snatched it back, causing it to spill and splatter all over my dress.

"What, are you *stupid?!*" I couldn't believe this. "Oh, my God, you ruined my dress! You just dumb! Who invented you? Dang, you . . . get . . . on . . . my . . . nerves! Why don't you take I-95 and ride you and yo' gold tooth back down south. Uggggg! What crime did I commit to get hooked up with you?!" I hated being so mean, but didn't he ask for it? Looking at Melvin, I could tell I hurt his feelings because for the first time tonight he was silent.

"Yo," Josiah snapped, releasing his hands from around Deeyah's waist and standing up straight. "I think you owe my man an apology."

"Apology? If anything, you need to apologize for being up in my business!" I shouted. "Ain't nobody talkin' to you!"

"You know what?" Josiah said with extreme base in his voice. "You gotta nasty attitude. And I really don't know what it's for, 'cause you look ridiculous, rockin' a buncha knockoff. If you so miserable, why don't you take ya fat ass home!"

Every tear I had in my body filled my mouth, which is why I couldn't speak. Yaanah and Ki-Ki were looking around the club as if they hadn't heard anything. When I looked at Deeyah, she'd covered her lips with her right hand and a snide smile was sneaking out the side. Shae was standing there in disbelief, looking at Josiah as if at any moment she was about to give it to him. "You know I got yo' back," she said.

I wanted to cry so badly, but I'd been played out enough and if I let this slide, then all of them standing here would think they had the upper hand. So, this is what I did—I blacked on all of 'em. Straight up, I was 'bout to read 'em. "Deeyah, Yaanah, and Ki-Ki, I know y'all ain't laughin'." I looked at Shae for confirmation. "Should I get 'em, gurl?"

"Get 'em, gurl, 'cause I'ma get ole boy over here when you done." She placed her hand on her right hip and looked toward Josiah.

I snapped my neck. "Let me set you on fire real quick. We 'spose to be homegirls and y'all standin' here laughin', when everybody here know you three are the queens of knock off. If it wasn't for y'all, the Ten-Dollar Store woulda been closed down! You Payless-Target-Wal-Mart-havin'-Salvation Army freaks. Look like you get ya clothes out the Red Cross box. And word is, Josiah, you buy all of Deeyah's gear, so what that make you?"

"A hot-ass mess." Shae rolled her eyes in delight. "Looks like you been shut down, Superman."

"Whew, look at you girl," Melvin said, looking at Shae. "I likes me some aggressive women. Maybe I oughta hollar you. What's your name?"

"Boy, please," Shae said.

Josiah shot me a snide smile. "Your mouth is ridiculous." He eyed Deeyah and the expression on his face seemed to dance in laughter. "Y'all shot out."

"I don't believe you went there, Seven," Deeyah said. "You know Ki-Ki ain't boostin' from the Red Cross box no more."

"Don't be tryna call me out!" Ki-Ki shouted. "That was Yaanah's idea anyway."

"Oh, no, you didn't . . . !"

And the next thing I knew, these three were in a brawl over whose idea it was to jack the donation-clothing bin. But hmph, I didn't care. What difference did it make to me when I felt like the whole club was still trippin' off how bad Josiah played me. I knew it was time for me to roll, I just didn't want it to seem like I was running from something, or better yet, someone. "I'm not beat for this." I managed to keep the tears that flooded my mouth at bay. I turned to Melvin. "My fault if I hurt your feelings."

"Oh, you ain't hurt my feelings, Shawtie. That just turned me on."

If I didn't feel like crying, I would've laughed. "I'm 'bout to bounce."

"Hold up, Seven," Shae called behind me. "'Cause I'm 'bout to bounce with you."

And just like *America's Next Top Model*, we threw our right shoulders forward, our bootylicious oceans in motion and proceeded out the door.

2

My body was buried beneath a heap of pink covers when I stretched my left arm out and slapped the snooze button on my alarm clock. I had it programmed so I would wake up to Jay-Z and Beyoncé singing "Upgrade U." Up until last night, nobody could tell me this wasn't me and Josiah's jam, but since he tried to play me, "Irreplaceable" was now our song.

I let my arm swing on the side of my twin-sized bed and drop to the floor. I needed at least five more minutes of sleep. Getting up at six o'clock in the morning was the worst, especially when I had a pain-in-the-behind ten-year-old brother called Man-Man and a sixty-year-old throwback cousin named Shake, who made it his business to scare me every morning wearing too-tight MC Hammer pants, a polyester muscle shirt, high top L.A. Gears, and a pair of DMC Gazelles.

"Make it do what it do!" Cousin Shake yelled from behind our bedroom door.

"Fat Mama!" Man-Man pounded like 5-O. "Wake . . . yo' . . . big butt . . . jelly roll . . . on the pole . . . roach-lookin' self up! And tell two dollar lil' Kim to get up, too!"

"Toi," I growled, turning my head toward my sister's bed. "I'ma kill 'im."

"Retardos!" Man-Man banged again. "The special ed bus outside!"

"Make it do what it do, now!" Cousin Shake said as if he were waiting for a response. "Fat Mama and Toi, is ya dead? Answer me!" He pounded. "Let Cousin Shake know if ya dead so I'll know what to tell yo' mama when she calls and wanna know why y'all ain't up yet. Po' mama, out there workin' the graveyard shift at the phone company and y'all around here makin' tricks of yourselves. This exactly why I don't think ya need to be going out anyway. If it was up to me, you'd have supper by five and be in the bed by eight! You might be foolin' ya mama, but I can see right through ya, out there gyratin' ya'selves for a buncha ex-convicts. That's right, I said it ex . . . con . . . victs. Now, get up fo' I call the law on ya! Y'all gon' get some education 'round here!"

"In case you didn't know"—I snatched the door open—"I fight old people."

"Anytime, anyplace, lil' girl, 'cause the day you

hit me is the day I'm gon' teach you what rock and roll is all about. Now, get ready for school, fo' Cousin Shake have to handle you."

"Calm down, Cousin Shake." Man-Man had a smug look on his face. "You ain't got to deal with this. I'm just gon' tell Mommy on 'em!"

All I could do was roll my eyes and slam the door in their face. "Toi, I swear I can't stand them. Why did Cousin Shake have to come here to live after his wife died? God, he gets on my nerves!"

I started rummaging through my closet for something to wear. "Toi!" I called, realizing she didn't answer me. "Toi!!" Still no answer. As I walked over to her bed, I heard a knock at my bedroom window. I pulled the curtains back and there she was, gawkin' at me with a cheesy smile about a mile wide. "You . . . must be . . . stupid!" I opened the window to let her in. "Mommy told you the next time she even *hears* about you sneaking in through the window, she was gon' put bars on it, and I'm sorry sistah girl, but I'm not tryna be in jail."

"Nobody said you had to be in jail." She fell from the window to the floor. "All in my business!"

"Ah un rudeness." I couldn't believe this. "Are those words I hear comin' out the side of yo' neck?! 'Cause I swear on all the love I have for Bow Wow, honey dip, I will rock you to sleep. Know what? I'm just gon' tell Mommy 'cause I'm tired of this."

"What you mean, tell Mommy? You want us

both to be on lockdown? If you do that, you know she not gon' wanna hear about you going to no more parties, no more staying up late, and you know the phone'll be comin' outta here."

I hated it when she made sense. "I'm getting real sick of you. You gon' mess around and get into some trouble you can't get out of." I started rummaging through my closet for school clothes again. "And I hope you had some sleep, because Cousin Shake's disability kicked in, so he stopped working at Wal-Mart. And his miserable self is here all day, looking for a reason to scream on us. Besides, school just started and you've already skipped like five times. And if you do it *again,* Mommy is gon' flip and that will be on you and not on me." I pulled out a pair of tight Baby Phat jeans, a hot pink tee with "The definition of fresh" written in rhinestones across the front, pink bangles, and matching hoop earrings. "You need to tell Qua to stop keeping you out all night."

"Okay, Mother," she remarked sarcastically. "And for your information, I planned on going to school today."

"You need to go everyday. Keep it up and you won't be graduating."

"Anywho, since when Cousin Shake stop working at Wal-Mart?"

"Since I started minding my business," he yelled through the door.

Toi and I looked at each other and fell out laughing.

Before Qua came along, I loved being around my sister. We were fraternal twins and we used to be best friends until her taboo boyfriend came along.

Word on the street is that he's a street pharmacist, which is part of the reason my sister is draped in Purple labels and Bebe all the time. I haven't said anything about it, because I don't want Toi to flip on me. But I know if my mother ever hears wind of this, it'll be the end of these two as we know it.

And to make matters worse, my mother doesn't know he's twenty. Toi lied and told her he was eighteen and attended Essex County College. He used to come around until Cousin Shake started yelling, "Take cover!" every time he walked through the door.

Now, Toi goes over to his place and spends every waking moment she can with him. He has a small house he flipped over on Nye and there've been plenty of times I've seen girls coming in and out of his spot, a few of them even riding around with him in his car. Once, I told Toi what he was doing and peep this, homegirl went right back and told him exactly what I said. Every freakin' word. And after he lied and made her think I was hatin' on her, who did Toi accuse of making things up? Me. Not Qua. But me. I was pissed and from that moment on, I swore she would never hear another word about Ghetto Charming from these divafied lips.

"I got bathroom first!" I ran out the room, leaving her sitting on the bed, still laughing at Cousin Shake.

By the time I was showered, dressed, and back in the room, she was under the covers sleeping. "You better get up," I snapped, spraying oil sheen in my hair.

"I got cramps," she said groggily.

"You should've had cramps last night. Come on, Toi, I'm not doing any more work for you."

"Then don't," she snapped. "Go. I'll meet you there." She turned over and buried her head beneath the pillow.

"Whatever." I looked in the mirror and applied my MAC lip gloss. "If you want Qua to pimp you the rest of your life, then you do boo. 'Cause if you keep acting like this, I won't have to tell Mommy—you'll be forced to. Stupid!" Before I left, I snatched the covers off her.

"What took you so long, Bubble Butt?!" Man-Man said, sitting at the table finishing up his grits.

"He's the only respectable one 'round here." Cousin Shake patted my brother on the head. I started to say something but watching Cousin Shake's pants rise up his butt was better than thinking of a sarcastic comeback.

I sat down to the table and Cousin Shake began fixing me a bowl of grits as if he were slopping oatmeal in a soup kitchen.

"Butter?" he asked.

"Yes."

18

"Salt?"

"Sugar, please." I was trying to be nice.

"That's what wrong witcha now," he snorted, while sporting the biggest wedgie I'd ever seen. "You too damn sweet." He sprinkled two teaspoons of sugar over the butter in my grits. "Who ever heard of sugar in grits?"

"You love me, don't you, Cousin Shake?"

"Crazy 'bout you." He kissed me on the forehead. "Now, where is Toi? She going to school if I gotta punch her in the face and make her do it."

"I hear you, Cousin Shake!" Toi yelled as she dragged herself to the bathroom.

"Cousin Shake love ya, gurl! You know I do."

As usual, all I could do was laugh at Cousin Shake. Don't get me wrong, there were times where I wanted to choke him, but I knew he cared. Just sometimes he cared a little too much.

"Hur' up, Fat Mama. Yo' lil' brain need all the education it can get."

I didn't even respond. I finished my grits, mushed Man-Man in the head, and walked out the door.

3

It was the end of September and the weather was different everyday. Some days were sixty and seventy degrees and others ranged anywhere from the low forties to fifties, but today blew it all out the water . . . it was a record-breaking eighty-five degrees. Somebody—somewhere—had treated Brick City to a surprise summer day—which meant one thing: everybody and their mama were outside, even at seven-thirty in the morning.

We were from the southward section of Newark, New Jersey, reppin' for South 14th Street, where everybody knew everybody and you could always count on somebody being all in your business.

When I stepped onto the porch, the sun starting baking my face and Ciara's "Goodies" was blasting from an unknown radio somebody had placed in their front window. I waved at my neighbors, who lived on both sides of me and across the street. Most of them were old people or my friends' grandparents, who were either sitting on their steps or chillin' on their porches in plastic lounge chairs, old recliners, or worn love seats. The bus stop was crowded with school kids and parents going to work, and the corner bodega was buzzing with customers coming in and out.

Toi still hadn't made her way out the house, but at least she was up and getting dressed. Right about now, my mother was due to come home from work for a few hours before heading to her second job as a part-time bus driver for New Jersey Transit. And if she sees homegirl still in the crib lollygagging around, I know she's gon' flip, especially since she hasn't been pleased with Toi's nasty attitude lately. The daily speech after school has become a battle of who's the mother and who's the child. I feel like "I had you, you didn't have me" is Toi's middle name.

"Ballin'!!" Shae yelled our clique's greeting while snapping her fingers in a zigzag motion as she headed up the block to meet me. "What's really hood, boo?" She smiled, while checking out my gear.

"I see you peepin' me, homegirl." I placed my hands on my hips. "I'm just too hot for words."

"But hot is what we do best." She placed her backpack on the ground and began working it out. "Please, feel me." She pointed to her chest. "Ms. RaShaeyah Harris is sportin' "—she strutted in front of my porch as if she were on the catwalk—"denim capris with Apple Bottoms written across the boo . . . ty, a sweet pink Apple Bottoms party tee, a midriff hoodie . . . and please peep the rhinestone-studded Apple Bottoms sneakers. Now give it up, give me my props, please." Her silver bangles clapped together as she started to vogue.

"Oh, whatever." I rolled my eyes. "You know we stay fly." At least that's what I always wanted to believe. And it's not that I didn't think I was cute or I had no confidence in myself, it's just that I always felt fat . . . huge is more like it . . . and although it's cool when it's just me and Shae . . . when we all get together, I feel like the biggest girl in the world, especially when my friends are rockin' something I could never touch: a belly shirt, cargo catsuit, or some super tight slinky J-Lo gear . . .

All my life I've been cute and chubby. Toi was slender and sexy with big boobs. Growing up, we were called, Fat Mama and Lil' Mama, which I hated because it was a constant reminder of what I couldn't stand most about myself.

Believe it or not, I didn't always know I was reppin' fo' the big girls. I can remember being in the mall with my mother and her asking someone if The Children's Place had plus sizes. Hmph. I turned to her and said, "Who you buying that for?"

But then the revelation came. My cousins and I were all going to Bowcraft with my aunt and her boyfriend. We were so excited, making plans to ride everything we saw in the amusement park. And when it came time for us to go, my aunt's boyfriend said, "Fat Mama, make sure you sit in the middle to help the tires balance the car." I was devastated and all I can remember thinking was, *I can't believe I'm big enough to balance a car. I must be humongous.*

My mother told him off when I told her what happened, but it never erased how I felt about myself.

I see on TV, ever since Tyra Banks gained weight and Mary Kate overdosed on starvation, that skinny is supposed to be out and thick is in, but I think it's a fad.

"Girl, Seven," Shae carried on. "People just got to see us to believe how funky, fresh, fly we are."

"Okay, Shae." I laughed, stepping off my porch. "That's enough of feeling yourself."

As we headed up the block toward the bus stop, "You look nice, RaShaeyah," floated from behind us. When we turned around, we saw it was Shae's mother smiling at us, looking as if she hadn't changed her clothes in weeks. I knew Shae was embarrassed, especially since she told me she and her mother made a pact that if anybody was around they weren't to speak, but maybe this time her mother forgot. I guessed that's why nobody else ever knew exactly who Shae's mother was, except me. But I didn't care, Shae was my girl no matter what. After all, her mother was on drugs, she wasn't.

"I shoulda let my daddy take me to school,"

Shae mumbled. Her father was who she and her two brothers lived with.

"Hey." Shae's mother smiled at me.

I waved. I didn't know what to say. What kinda conversation do you hold with a crack fiend?

"I saw y'all over there profiling," Shae's mother carried on. "Y'all look real, real cute, too."

"Uhmm hmm," Shae responded.

"Okay, well, I won't hold you . . . too long." She gave Shae half a grin.

"Here." Shae slid something in her mother's hand. "Let's go, Seven." We rushed past her and ran to the bus stop to catch the oncoming bus.

"What'd you hand her?" I asked, as we stepped onto the bus.

"Two dollars. I didn't wanna see her beggin' for it."

"Shawtie!!" Melvin yelled as soon as me and Shae walked through the school's doors. I hadn't even made it down the hallway good and already he was harassing me. I looked around and there was no place to run. Truth be told, I wanted to steal on him, make him punch drunk, and then maybe he'd leave me alone. "Look at you, gurl." He squinted his nose and looked me up and down. "All decked out, like you the ace of spades."

"Do I know you?" I squinted my eyes.

"You better know yo' man." He gave me a hug without asking. "Shawtie, you just the type woman I need." He squeezed. "Know how to fill a man up." He let me go. "I can look at you and tell somebody in yo' house know how to cook."

I could tell that Shae was doing her all not to laugh.

"Look at you," he growled, "all fine and er'thang. Girl, if you were a cake I'd lick all . . . yo' . . . icing off."

"Melvin, just when I was about to apologize, you just keep carrying on."

"You ain't heard? Apologies turn me on."

Am I dreaming?

"You wanna introduce me?" my sister asked as she and a group of her friends stood by. Seeing her in school must've been how I realized this was real.

"You cool," I said. "You don't need any introductions."

"This family?" Melvin butted in. "Come on, now. You kin to Shawtie?"

"This is my baby sister. Well, we're twins, but I'm the oldest." Toi extended her hand. I could tell she was trying to be funny. "You must be new here."

Now . . . why . . . did she say that? I knew the performance was coming. And sure enough, he cupped his hands on both sides of his mouth, leaned back, and shouted out, "MUR . . . FREES . . . BORO!! Dirty-dirty in the house. I'm Melvin, but my pot'nahs call me Big Country."

All I could do was shake my head.

"So what's ya name, sistah-in-law?"

Sistah-in-law?

"Toi."

"Whew-wee, y'all got some names on y'all. You named Toi, ya sistah named Seven, what's ya mama's name? Jump Off?"

I started rummaging through my purse. *I think I brought a blade to school.*

"Bye, Seven." Toi smiled as she and her friends laughed on their way to class. "Bye, Shae, and bye, Big Country."

"Don't be no stranger!" Melvin yelled. "Come see us again."

"Ballin'!!" I heard coming up the hallway. I knew it was Deeyah and the rest of the get-along gang: Ki-Ki and Yaanah. They must've missed the hint last night, because I'm not speaking to them. I rolled my eyes as they stopped in front of my locker.

"Dang, Shawtie." Melvin was in my business again. "You still mad at yo' crew? Don't be like that. You know you being mad turns me on and I got Sex Ed first period. I might go in decent and come out a freak."

I'm not sure if anyone saw me, but I had passed out.

"Big Country!!" One of Melvin's friends shouted from the other end of the hall. "Yo, that's my dawg. He from ATL. Y'all better watch out, the dirty-dirty 'bout to take over. I'll see you at three o'clock, Shawtie!" He winked his eye and ran toward his friends.

I looked toward Shae. "If I give you a knife, will you stab him?"

She laughed. "You better stop sleeping on Big Country. He's a cutie with his big sexy self."

"Big? Sexy? He looks like I could fry chicken on him."

"Well, fry me some please? 'Cause all I see is fine."

"Your taste in boys is the worst. I almost forgot you thought Mike Jones was cute."

"What, you ain't know. Plus, my auntie says one thing about a southern man is he keeps a job."

"I'd rather they be unemployed."

"So"—Deeyah cleared her throat—"do y'all not see us standing here?"

"I see you workin' my nerves," I snapped.

"And I see you, but I don't hear no apologies comin' outcha mouth." Shae sucked her teeth. "So, until then, you need to step." She flicked her hand as if she'd just completed a magic trick.

"Excuse me, Shug Knight." Deeyah rolled her eyes at Shae. "But what I'ma apologize for? We all know Seven was mistreating Melvin."

"So what?" I jumped in. "You 'spose to be my girl and you were 'spose to have my back, but instead you were stuck underneath Josiah like some lil' played-out groupie."

"You just mad 'cause he called you fat."

"Exactly."

"But you played us by leaving us standing there," Deeyah said.

"What was she 'spose to do?" Shae snapped. "Stand there for more insults?"

"Look," Ki-Ki added her two cents. "Y'all three need to make up. You know we swore no boy was gon' ever come between the Hottie posse."

"Girl, please," I said. "We ain't the Hottie posse. We lil' Divas, so be gone."

"Booyah," Shae said.

I could tell they wanted to laugh. Ki-Ki smiled. "Seven and Shae"—she playfully twisted her lips—"bump Josiah and Melvin and all the rest of them. We been girls since elementary school and we need to remember that."

"You must've written that down last night," Shae said, "cause I ain't impressed. Just know that the next time, we gon' throw."

I looked at her. "Why you always wanna beat somebody up?" We all fell out laughing.

"Look, let's blow this popsicle stick," Deeyah said, "and be girls again. I know it's only been a night, but I miss my two Pooh-Poohs." She pinched our cheeks.

"Ai'ight," Shae and I said reluctantly. "I guess we can be girls again."

As we started talking about going out this week-end, Dollah walked by and grabbed Deeyah's hand. "What's good, papi?" She winked her eye.

Dollah was short for Million Dollah—a nickname he gave himself because he bragged all over the school that he had a million dollar basketball game. His real name was Clyde Gatling Jr., which he hated to be called. He was the spitting image of Omarion, who I thought was cute but Shae said looked like a broke-down Snoop, minus the perm. Dollah was tall, slim, and had bronze-colored skin. He was center position on the basketball team and was second in popularity and fineness behind Josiah. Which was why I was so blinded by flatter when he showed interest in me last year, gave me his class ring (which I keep forgetting to give back to him), and asked me to be his girl. And at the time, I really liked him, especially since everybody else had a boyfriend and I wanted one, too. The only thing was he never wanted anybody in school to know he was my man. He never paid me any attention in school, only came to my house once in a blue moon or should I say every full moon, and come to find out not only was he seeing half the girls in the school, he was lying to some of the kids around our way that he was pimping me for booty and that I was trickin' all my Burger King money on him. So, to say the least, I dumped him. One day he spoke to me and I stopped talking to him. Simply kept it movin'. He would call my house and I would hang up on him. Eventually he got the hint and now we have an understanding: *Don't say nothing to me and I won't have to slap you.*

And that's not the half of it. Josiah and Dollah are archenemies, so what Deeyah was doing holding Dollah's hand was beyond me. Pretty much Josiah and Dollah are like Shaq and Kobe. They can't stand one another and everybody knows it. Last year these two got into a great big fight, when

Josiah intercepted a pass meant for Dollah and made the state championship's winning basket. Dollah bum-rushed him and snuck him from the back. The entire gym was in an uproar and what made it worse was that the college scouts were there, recruiting some of the senior players and keeping their eyes on the junior ones.

But for real-for real, I think that the basketball thing is a cover-up for why they really don't like each other. The real deal, I think, is because of their brothers. Josiah had an older brother, Ibn, and he was best friends with Dollah's brother, Best. Well, no one knows the real deal. All we know is what the paper reported, and that was Ibn and Best stole a car, they were being chased by the police, the car spun out of control, and Ibn died. Now Dollah's brother is in jail doing football numbers for Ibn's murder. So you see, Josiah and Dollah were destined to be enemies. Therefore, what Josiah's girl was doing holding hands with his archrival was beyond me. All I knew is I didn't wanna be around when it all went down.

"When you coming to see about me, ma?" Dollah asked Deeyah, looking her up and down.

Oh heck, no he didn't?! I don't care if nobody knew we actually went together, how was he gon' play me and be in my friend's face?

"Why?" She smacked her lips. "What you got for me?"

"Why don't you come after school and find out?" he said.

"I gotta wait at least until my mother is asleep."

"Bet," he said to Deeyah but looked at me out the corner of his eye. "Stay sweet, ma, 'cause I gotta senior ring I need to get for you."

"You should have two," I snapped. " 'Specially since this your second time in twelfth grade."

"Dang, Dollah, you that smart?" Deeyah asked. "They keep calling you back, huh?"

"You know how I do it," Dollah said as he walked away.

We all just looked at Deeyah and shook our heads. "Am I on *That's So Raven* and Chelsea has come to life?" Shae snapped in disbelief.

"You being real sexist, Shae." Deeyah batted her eyes. "I'm real surprised at you."

"I swear to God, I'ma scream!"

"Anyway," I said. "Deeyah, so what's this with you and Dollah? Did I miss something?"

"What?" Deeyah was grinning from ear to ear.

"What's all that meet me after school and carrying on? What you 'spose to be?"

"Nothing."

"Well, it sure didn't look like nothing," Shae said. "It look like a jump-off contest."

"You cheating on Josiah?" I asked in disbelief.

"And why are you so concerned with what I'm doing with Josiah?" Deeyah snapped. "And there ain't gon' be too many more jump-offs, Shae."

"Good." Shae smirked. "Give the male population a rest."

"That was really racist, Shae."

The first period bell went off and we all headed to homeroom for attendance. I passed by Josiah as I walked down the hall and instantly I started feeling like a fool all over again. For the first time, he looked me in my eyes and smiled. I wanted to flip him the bird and smack him but instead I waved my hand and kept it moving. Had I looked at him too long I would've returned his smile.

Although I was in honors classes, it didn't mean I never got bored. *So what Josiah was doing standing in the doorway ignoring the teacher and coming over to talk to me, I didn't know. I tried to act like I didn't see him. Instead, I continued to do what I always did, which was write his name a thousand different ways in my notebook: bubble letters, cursive, fancy print, and matching my first name with his last name, all with hearts encircling them. "I'm so sorry"—he slipped my pen out of my hand—"about the way I treated you, Seven. Please accept my apology."*

"Yes, of course I will."

He lifted me out of my chair, ran his fingers through my hair, and just as he went to tell me he wasn't feeling anyone but me, the school bell rang and it was time to change classes. I hate daydreams!

I looked down at my notebook and instead of class notes, I had Josiah's name written all over my pages. I looked around my class as if I'd just returned from space. I had no idea what had gone on in there, but as we were on our way out, the teacher announced, "Quiz on today's topic tomorrow."

Jesus . . .

I thought I had my *Romeo and Juliet* book for English class in my backpack, but I didn't. It must've been in my locker. I had three minutes to go to my locker, get it, and return before Mrs. Flinch threw a fit about me being late, so I took off running down the hall, dodging through the students like they were a maze, and just when I thought I'd made it through with ease, I ran right into Josiah, knocking everything out of my hand and practically pushing him to the floor. As if I hadn't been embarrassed enough, now he'll say I was so fat I almost knocked him down.

"My fault." I hated that I couldn't avoid checking him out, but he was so fine, who could resist? He wore a pair of baggy black Enyce jeans, a white tee with the Superman emblem in the middle, but instead of having the letter S in it, it had the letter J, an oversize belt buckle, and fresh Jordans on his feet.

I hurried and picked up my things off the floor.

"Dang, you got somethin' against being helped?" he asked, handing me my notebook, the one with his name scribbled in it.

I looked at him and smirked. "Nah, my fat ass

can do it." I snatched my notebook out his hand and practically tripped the rest of the way to my locker.

I grabbed the book I needed and slammed my locker shut. As I turned around to head to class, Josiah was leaning against the wall directly across from me with his North Face backpack thrown over one shoulder and his right foot propped behind him against the wall. "Yo ma, for real, you lookin' kinda right in them jeans."

I almost stuttered, but I caught myself. "Funny, that didn't sound like an apology."

"It wasn't. It was a compliment."

Dang, what happened to my mean mug? Why was I smiling?! "This the first time you seen me in jeans?"

"Nah." He licked his sexy lips. "But this the first time I'm tellin' you about it."

My heart dropped and for a moment I couldn't breathe. "Whatever." I turned away from him and threw my switch into overdrive as I proceeded down the hall.

"Oh, you playin' dirty? In a minute I'ma be apologizing to the wrong part of you."

I batted my eyes and turned around. "What could Mr. All-Star have done that would require him to apologize . . . to me?"

"We both know why I should apologize. So you need to go ahead on and accept it. 'Cause technically you owe me one, too."

Jesus, why do I love him? "Yeah, you wait on that apology." I sucked my teeth. "Plus, look at how you act toward me!"

"How do I act?" He walked over to me and his breath smelled sweet as it blew across my face.

I was too nervous to step back. "Josiah, you are always nasty to me. And for as long as I've ever known you, you've played me crazy."

"But look at how you do me . . . and I'ma upperclassman. You supposed to have some respect." He laughed. "But for real, though. Half the time you don't speak and when you do, it's because you thought of new words you wanna try and cuss me out with. I'm sayin', ma"—he pushed my shoulder-length hair behind my ears—"can ya boy get a break?"

My boy, more like my man.

Please do not ask me how, but him pushing my hair back made me lose control of my backpack and everything in my hand fell to the floor. My English book slid down the hall and my notebook with his name scribbled in it flew open at his feet. We both looked down at the same time and I just knew he saw his name drawn a million times with hearts all over them. He bent down, picked up my notebook, and handed it to me. I was so nervous that I snatched it and practically ran down the hall to pick up my English book. I didn't know whether to turn around and face him or not, so I started walking toward my class.

"Slow up, beautiful. You don't have to run." He

grabbed my waist from behind and twirled me around toward him. "It's cool." He ran his left hand across my cheek and my dimples lit up.

In a minute, I'ma hyperventilate!

I was cheesing so hard I hadn't even noticed Deeyah standing in front of us. She tapped the heel of her stiletto riding boot. "My eyes must be deceiving me, Josiah, 'cause I know you not hustling backwards!" She pointed her finger and rolled her eyes. "What is this, Seven? You tryna be me?"

"And why would I do that?" I snapped. "Then I'd be standing there looking at my man playing me."

"How could you be looking at yourself? When you gon' catch a hint, he don't want you?!"

"I can't tell"—I rolled my neck—"he was in my face and not once did he mention yo' behind!"

Josiah looked at me sideways, but I didn't care. I didn't know what type of game these two were playing but I'm not the one. "Y'all can leave me outta this nonsense." I rolled my eyes and started to walk away. Josiah snatched me back by my forearm and I felt forced to stand still. *Why was this turning me on?*

"Don't do that, ma," he said. "Don't kick a buncha ying yang and then take off like what you said was the end-all. 'Cause obviously you two got it twisted. I'm not no lil' boy and I'm not beat for nonsense, so you running off at the mouth like you tryna be saved and you gettin' all amped up like you 'bout to do something"—he pointed to

Deeyah—"you better dead that, 'cause I ain't the one. I can kick it to who I wanna kick it to, and I don't have to ask your permission."

"Josiah—" she attempted to interrupt.

"I'm talking. And you know what we talked about, so chill. And unless you wanna be embarrassed, you'll step back to class." He turned to me. "Your mouth is ridiculous and that's the part of you I'm not feeling, so kill it." He looked me up and down and swaggered down the hall.

It took everything in me not to skip behind him and say, "Okay, Daddy."

I looked at Deeyah and gave her a look that dared her to say something. For a moment, I couldn't remember why we were even friends this long. Maybe it had something to do with the ridiculous pact we made in elementary school or something like that. But right about now, I could tell that all bets were about to be off.

4

Never know when you might stop by . . .

—FANTASIA, "WHEN I SEE YOU"

"**N**ow why you wanna see me fight?" Shae snapped as she rang up her customer and I bagged for mine. We worked at Burger King in Livingston Mall after school for four hours every other day and on the weekends. And we rarely called in sick unless there was a party or a game we wanted to attend.

"Fight? For what?" I handed my customer their food. "You love to brawl, don't you? I'm glad we're friends."

"Oh, you my girl," Shae assured me while handing her customer their receipt. "We down like a broke ho, but the rest of ya little Hottie posse, we shoulda left them behind when Deeyah became a ditzy jump-off. And Ki-Ki, oh, my God, if she tells the guidance counselor another story about how her mother's a crackhead and that's why she can't do her homework, I'ma smack her. And Yaanah, she ai'ight when she's by herself, but when she gets around Deeyah, she breaks fly too much."

"Dang, so why you hang around them?"

"I don't hang with them, me and you hang, and them heifers just posse fillers. They can be replaced."

"You a trip."

"But on the real, sometimes you just outgrow certain people. My daddy told me that true friends don't come along that often. That's why you my girl and the others . . . I can take 'em or leave 'em."

"Ohhhh," I whined. "Boo-Boo, you love me?"

"Stop sweatin' yourself."

"Oops." I laughed as I rang up another customer and handed them their food.

"But on the real"—Shae laughed—"let me ask you a question."

"What?"

"How do you feel with Josiah being homegirl's dude and you on him? Like, you my girl and all, but that seem kinda shady, right?"

"Yeah . . . I guess, but he came at me. I would've never stepped to him. Besides, look at how she all on Dollah and you know they gettin' it in."

"But she ain't know about you and Dollah. Besides, you don't even like Dollah."

"So, it's the principle."

"But she could say the same thing."

"Oh well, charge it to the game, 'cause I'm on him."

Shae laughed. "You so wrong."

"Besides, heck, who knows? Maybe Josiah was just being nice."

"Nice? Girl, please. Nice is 'How are you' or 'You look pretty.' Not stroking your cheek and running his fingers through your hair That's 'I'ma tryna see you.' "

"So, should I feel bad . . . about Deeyah?"

"Nope. You know we gettin' tired of her anyway. Always thinking she better than somebody 'cause her father's a city councilman. Besides, does she act like a friend to you with all the slickness she be saying? 'You look cute for a big girl' and all of that. Girl, you better than me, 'cause I woulda cussed that airbag out a long time ago."

"So, if you felt that way, why did you ask me how I felt with Josiah being in my face?"

"Just to be askin'."

I could tell she was lying. "Why did you ask?"

"No reason." She laughed.

"Don't lie."

"Ai'ight, what if . . ."—she stalled—"I told you I was kinda checkin' for . . ."

"For who?"

"Don't laugh . . . if you laugh I'm not telling you nothing else."

"Who?" I pressed.

"Melvin."

"Melvin? M-e-l-v-i-n? Big Country? You checkin'
for Big Country?" I couldn't believe this. "His zits
glow in the dark."

"No, they don't! Besides, we all have a lil' acne
problem every now and then, and if you look at
him, his face cleared up."

"I can't believe we're having this discussion." I
wiped my brow.

"And if you look at him real good he looks like
Chris Brown."

"You mean Bobby Brown."

"Oh, yeah, Bobby is cute."

"Ill."

"I'm just playing." Shae smiled. "But I think
Melvin's fine. Plus, I like big boys."

"Okay, Shae. Actually, he's not ugly." I swallowed
deeply. This was a stretch even for me. "But he is
country and you gon' mess around and he gon'
have you in Murphy-freakin'-boro on the corner
of the farm, pimpin' you."

"You so stupid." She laughed. "But yeah, I think
he's cute and he can dress."

"Yeah, he be throwin' it on, but hmph, he is so
not my type."

"Excuse me, Mr. Twenty-three ain't exactly all
that now—"

"What? You don't think he's fine?"

"He ai'ight, but every time I look at him I see
Nelly. And every time I see Nelly, all I hear is,
'Drop down and getcha eagle on gurl!' You gon'
be gettin' yo' eagle on, Seven?"

"I will slap you."

Shae laughed. "Plus, Josiah kinda irks my nerves."

"Josiah gets on your nerves but you can toler-ate Melvin?"

"Exactly, so you tryna see Melvin or what?"

"You wanna push up?"

"If you ai'ight with that."

"Girl, please. Matter-fact, I'ma hook y'all up. Don't even worry. The next time he shouts 'Yo Shawtie,' he gon' be talking to you."

"Seven—"

"For real, I got you Shae—"

"Would you shut up?! Cuties at five o'clock!"

When I looked to my right it was Josiah and about three of the sexiest lil' daddies I'd ever seen in my life. Two went to our school and one of them I'd never seen before. I can't believe he drove all the way up here to see me!

I looked at Shae, who was grinnin' so hard that if she moved, she would trip over her front teeth. "RaShaeyah, close your mouth."

I started chewing the gum I had stuck on the inside of my cheek. "Welcome to Burger King"—I popped a bubble—"where you can have it your way . . ." *I sound a hot mess.*

Josiah curled his top lip. "Hit me with a Sprite."

Hit him with Sprite . . . a Sprite . . . he did not just say hit him with a Sprite, 'cause right about now I will do it. Matter-fact, I should take my heart out and punch him in the face with it. I know he hears it beggin' to be his. I swear, I think

he just played me. He wasn't supposed to say,
"Hit me with a Sprite." He was supposed to say,
44 *"Can I get wit' you, Seven?" I had an answer for*
that, but now I stood speechless.

"Yo," he said as his eyes checked me out but his mouth sounded as if one of his homies died. "Let me get a large Sprite and some fries." His friends were in Shae's line, grinning like they'd found gold, and Shae was cheesin' so hard, I thought I would have to wipe the slob off the side of her mouth, especially when one of them asked for her number and she almost wrote it down on a French fry. "There are other customers in your line." At that moment, I was hatin' but I didn't care.

"You smell that?" she asked while continuing to smile.

"What?"

"Haterraid."

All I could do was laugh. "That'll be three eight five." I gave Josiah his total. He handed me the money, collected his change, and then he and his friends sat down at one of the tables. Before I could figure out if he came in to torture me or 'cause he was really hungry, I heard a little boy say, "Hey, Bubble Butt," followed by, "What it do, Fat Mama?" I knew that could only be two people, Man-Man and Cousin Shake. Oh . . . my . . . God . . . !

Shae placed her hand over her mouth. "Just write down a few words, but I'll give your eulogy."

Cousin Shake and Man-Man stood in front of me.

"What?" I said through clenched teeth. "Don't come in here tryin' to order pizza. We don't sell hotdogs, and no, we were never Red Lobster. So look at the menu board and place your order. And why you gotta be in my line?" I know I was pouring it on extra thick, but you should've seen these two clowns last week when they came in here, wanting a handheld menu and table service.

"Do I need to speak to a manager in this piece?" Cousin Shake said, as his muscle shirt was starting to creep over the two love handles around his waist. "What happened to the greetin'? Did they outlaw 'May I help you? Would you like fries with that shake?' Let me know now, otherwise I'ma have to handle you and find out the reason why you rollin' yo' eyes like you straight off a slave ship."

Why, God? When I looked at Josiah, he was staring at me, then he quickly diverted his gaze the other way.

" 'Cuse me?" Cousin Shake frowned. "I'm over here, that's ya problem, concentratin' on them funny lookin' boys over there! You better look at 'em and say, 'Not my goodies,' instead of smiling so hard. I ain't never seen boys with mo' hair than girls. Truth be told, when they got hair like that I start looking at how they holding their wrist. I see you over there, Shae. Don't think I won't get after you, too."

"Yeah, chicken-neck, we see you and Bubble Butt. We can't help but see you."

"Die already!" I said to Man-Man.

" 'Least my breath don't stink, dragon!"

I took a deep breath and did all I could not to fly over the counter. "Can I . . . take . . . your order please?"

"That's a lil' better," Cousin Shake said. "Now, let me see . . ." He looked at the menu board. "Y'all got Chinese chicken wings and gravy?"

All I could do was pound my fist on the counter. "This is Burger King!"

"That ain't answering my question."

"No."

"No, what?"

"We don't sell Chinese chicken wings and gravy!"

"Oh, then I'll have some fried gizzards."

"Yuck."

"We don't sell that, Cousin Shake," Shae said as she elbowed me. "Five o'clock," she mumbled.

"5-O?" Cousin Shake looked around. "You wanna call the cops on me? Do I need to get yo' mama up in here?"

I didn't even respond, I was too busy looking at Josiah and his friends, who were cracking up laughing at Cousin Shake. I was so embarrassed that embarrassed wasn't even the right word anymore.

"COUSIN SHAKE, WHAT IS YOUR ORDER?" I didn't mean to yell so loud, but I couldn't help it.

"I don't believe this!" He snorted. "Here"—he took off his glasses—"put these on and then tell me who in da hell you talkin' to? Tell me now.

Please tell me, so I can jump over that counter and turn Burger King out."

"Alright, I'm sorry, Cousin Shake."

"Thought so." He looked down at Man-Man and put his glasses back on. "I feel like I've been to work. I told you we shoulda went to Pathmark and bought some ground beef, eggs, and bread."

"Naw, Cousin Shake," Man-Man said, "that's how you make Egg McMuffins. Don't nobody want that."

Oh, my God, oh, my God, oh . . . my . . . God . . .

"Never mind," Cousin Shake said. "I don't want nothing. You want something, Man-Man?"

"Naw, let's go to McDonald's. I hear they sell shrimp over there." As they turned to leave, Josiah and his friends were dumping their trash. Josiah hit me with a peace sign on his way out . . . and I felt like falling over the counter.

Somebody pray for me . . .

On the bus ride home, all I could think about was Josiah. Shae thought I was reading too much into how he acted, but I didn't think so. Maybe he thought I was silly. Or maybe I weighed fifty pounds more than the girl of his dreams.

By the time I got home, I was exhausted. My heart had passed out at least three times and in my mind, I kept saying, *Yes, I love him. No, I can't stand him. Yes, I want him, no, I don't. Yes, he has a girlfriend, but she doesn't appreciate him . . .* and on and on it went. If I didn't know any better, I would swear I needed a cigarette.

Cousin Shake was stretched out on the couch

asleep, with the hem of his pants looking as if a flood had come through, his muscle shirt rolled completely over his beer belly, his glasses pulled down the bridge of his nose, and a *GQ* magazine laying on his chest.

48

I knew he would try to stay up and wait for me. He always does, especially since my mother's usually at work. He likes to make sure I'm here safe, eating dinner, taking a bath, finishing my homework, and before he says goodnight, he argues about how McDonald's is putting Burger King to sleep.

As I passed by my mother's room, I saw her in bed reading. What was she doing home? Immediately I wondered where the heck Toi was.

"Ma, don't you have to work?"

"I have days off."

"Why didn't you tell us?"

" 'Cause the last time I checked, I was the mama."

"Well, excuse me." I laughed.

"You're excused. Now come here. I feel like I haven't seen you in a month."

When I walked in her room, my brother was laying at her feet and I mushed him on the head.

"Monkey dog!" He looked at me and made a face.

"Ah un rudeness! But it's okay, 'cause that's how you act when you're adopted."

"All right now, Seven," Mommy said sternly. "And no, Amir. Before you ask, you were not adopted.

Now go take a bath and then you can come back for five minutes before you go to bed."

"Stupid!" he shouted in my face and ran out the room.

"Now, you," Mommy said, "how was your day?" Instantly my face lit up.

My mother stared at me for a moment. She took her glasses off and laughed. She was the prettiest person I knew. Most people said I was the spitting image of her, and for the first time, with the exception of her not having dimples, I could kind of see it. "Who is he?" She patted her bed for me to sit down. I hated that she could see right through me.

"Nobody." I scooted next to her and she put her arm around me.

"Fat Mama, are you telling me the truth?" She reached on her nightstand, grabbed her Pepsi, and started drinking it.

"No." I felt like the goofiest kid in the world.

"Then tell me. If you tell me, then I'll tell you."

"About what?!" I said, excited. "You got a boy-friend?! And I didn't do the hook-up? Man-Man and Cousin Shake are gon' die."

"I *do not* need you hooking me up, thank you. Trust me, divorcing your daddy is hard enough."

"Oh." I hated when she reminded me that my daddy was no longer around. I haven't seen him in over a year. His job relocated and so did he . . . California someplace. Besides, ever since he cheated on my mother and had another baby, I refused to talk to him. My daddy still calls every weekend trying to get me or my sister on the phone, but I avoid him and Toi is never home when he calls. Man-Man is the only one who gives him the time of day. "Then what is it?"

"Nope, tell me first."

I sighed. "Okay . . . okay . . . okay . . . okay . . ."

"Can you stop saying okay and talk?"

I took a deep breath. Finally, I was going to admit this to somebody other than Shae. "I think I'm 'bout to be married."

"What?!" Her soda flew out her mouth as if she were spraying air freshener,

"Not literally, Ma. God!"

"Oh." She grabbed a Kleenex and wiped her mouth. "Well, you better make me understand, because you're going to college and that's that. We're going on the black college tour and everything next year. I'm already packed. And no sex!"

"Huh? Where did that come from?"

"I just threw that in there. Now, who is he?"

"I don't even wanna tell you now."

"Would you tell me?" She laughed. "Okay, I'll try for five minutes to not be your mother."

"Uhmm hmm."

"What's his name?"

"Josiah . . ." I mumbled.

"Who?"

"Josiah . . ."

"Biblical name, very nice. Now, do I know him?"

"No, he goes to my school. But I've been knowing him since I was about eleven and he was thirteen. He's a senior now."

"A senior? Is he going to college?"

"I don't know."

"You better find out . . . otherwise, keep it movin'!"

"Maaaaaa . . . would you stop preachin' and listen? Didn't you say five minutes without you being my mother?"

"Okay, you got three minutes left. Now, is he saying you feel me after every other word?"

"No, he doesn't talk like that."

"Good. Is Cousin Shake gon' yell 'Take cover' when he comes in the house?"

"No."

"Is he smart?"

"I didn't ask to see his report card."

"Well, I need a copy."

"Maaaaa!"

"Alright." She laughed. "Now, on to the important stuff. Is he cute?"

"Ma . . . he's so fine," I said in the dreamiest voice I could muster up, "that I'm tempted to call him pretty."

She leaned back against her iron headboard. "That's the same thing I said about your daddy."

"Ill." I was disgusted. "Ma, please, stop the visual."

"Excuse you, your father is very handsome.

Anyway, back to Mr. Pretty. When am I meeting him and his mama . . . and daddy, if he has one."

"See Ma." Already I was embarrassed. "Why you gotta be swat team on him?"

" 'Cause you're my child."

"But you don't need to know all those people."

"Yes, I do," she assured me. " 'Cause if they're crazy, then he's crazy too. And we gon' get rid of the drama early."

"That ain't right, Ma. You don't even know the boy and already you thinking he might be crazy . . ." I fell out laughing. "Now, what's your news?"

"I'm going to be starting a new job so I can be home a little more."

Immediately all my laughing stopped. "Really? Did you tell my sister?"

"I haven't seen your sister."

"Did you call her cell phone?"

"Uhmm hmm, I sure did. I called her before I got home and she told me she was in the bed."

"Oh." *At least she didn't lie.*

"Don't you worry about your sister. Ya mama got this. Remember, I was sixteen before. Now go on and get ready for bed."

"I have to finish my homework first."

"Well then, do that and then go to bed."

"Alright." I practically flew out the room. I needed to call Toi before she climbs in the window tomorrow morning and catches a beat-down. As soon as I ran down the hall, I walked right into Man-Man, who stood there with a 7-Eleven Big Gulp cup filled with water and ice. And just as I went to scream, "Mommy!!!!!" he threw it . . . all . . . in . . . my . . . face . . .

All I could do was stand there. "I'm . . . gon' . . . kick yo' . . ."

5

Shoulda known better than to think I would leave . . .

—MONICA, "YOU SHOULD HAVE KNOWN BETTER"

"Seven, get up!" I did all I could to get my mother out of my dream with Josiah, but she wouldn't leave us alone. "Wake up, Seven." My hips shook. "Wake up!"

"Hmmm," I said groggily. I wanted to get back to dreamin', but instead I opened one eye slowly and looked at her.

"Where is your sister?"

"At the library." I turned over, pulled the covers over my head, and did all I could to drift back to sleep.

"Seven! Wake up!" She pulled the covers off.

"Ma!!" I sat up. "I didn't leave those dishes in the sink."

"Seven." She patted me on the cheek. "You're dream drunk. Wake up."

"I'm woke." I rubbed my eyes. "I'm up."

"It's two o'clock in the morning. Where is your sister?"

I looked at the clock for confirmation and then I looked at Toi's bed, which was empty. "She's sleep." I grabbed my pillow, put it over my face, and fell straight back onto the bed.

"Do you hear me talking to you?!"

"Ma, for real, I don't know." I mumbled under the pillow and my mother snatched it off.

"Let me tell you something." My mother placed her hands on her hips, squinted her eyes, and spoke while biting into her bottom lip. "Lie to me again and see what happens! Now *you* got two seconds to tell me where she is before I do an operation on you called beat-down! Now unless you wanna catch it, like you a woman off the street steppin' to me, you will tell me where she is by the time I count to two or else you will need assistance to breathe. One . . ."

"At Qua's over on Nye." *I hate I let her punk me!*

"What?! How long has this been going on? And what kind of mother would allow her eighteen-year-old son to have his sixteen-year-old girlfriend spend the night?!"

"That's a good question."

"You being smart?"

"No."

"Didn't think so. Now give me the exact address."

My eyes widened. "You not going over there?" I

knew Toi had asked for it, but dang, who wants their mother dragging them out of their boyfriend's house? I was embarrassed for her. I'd almost rather if Cousin Shake came and got me. At least I would know he was all talk, but my mother . . . there's no telling what she would do. "Ma, you're scaring me. You can't go over there. Do you see what time it is? You going on Nye . . . alone?"

"I'm not going alone."

"Well . . . who are you going with?"

"You."

I don't think so . . . not the kid. She had to be joking. "Ma, for real, who are you going with?"

My mother flipped on my bedroom light. "Get up!"

"Ma, can't we just call her and tell her to come home?"

"If I tell you to get up again, I'ma knock you straight through the next two years. And when I get over there and get a hold of this boy's mama, whooool, all of Newark is gon' know about me."

"Ma"—I stood up—"you don't understand." My heart was racing and my palms were sweaty. "You can't be going around Newark beating up people's mamas."

"Oh, yeah?" she said sarcastically. "Hmph, we gon' see. Y'all think I'ma joke. But let me tell you now I'm not losing ya'll to no streets."

"Maybe she's at the store."

"Shut up, Seven, 'cause all that's open this time of night are legs."

SHORTIE LIKE MINE

"But Maaaaaaaaa." I stomped my feet like I was five again. "He doesn't live with his mother. He lives alone." *I can't believe I let that slip out.*

"Alone? At eighteen?"

"Yes—no—yes." I was not doing well with covering up.

"Which is it?"

"He lives alone but he's not eighteen?"

"What?! How old is he?"

"Maaaa . . ."

"Girl" . . . By this time my mother's breath was hitting my nose and it didn't smell too good.

"Ma"—I covered my nose—"did you brush your teeth?"

My mother raised her hand back. "Ai'ight." I spit out his age. "He's twenty!"

"Twenty?! I'ma kill her. Let's go!"

"Well, if you gon' kill her, Ma, I don't want to go. Let me remember her the way she was."

She stood silent and shot me a dagger with her eyes. Three things I knew: when she stopped talking, gave me the evil eye, or started repeating herself, she was due to explode any minute. I started chewing the inside of my cheek. "Should I wear all black?" and then I gave a stupid laugh. I just thought I would say something to lighten the mood. It didn't work.

I begged my mother to call one of my uncles or all four of them but for some reason she thought she was G.I. Jane and that her taped-up bat had something to prove.

Nye was live when my mother parked her black
Ford Taurus in front of Qua's house. There were
people on practically every porch in his neighbor-
hood: dancing, smoking, and drinking. The blocks
were lined with folks of all ages—fiends, detec-
tives, and narcs. The bodega had pulled down its
steel gates and was now selling loose cigarettes
and candy through bulletproof glass and a turn-
around. Half of the street lamps seemed to be taking the night off . . . and here was my mother,
Captain Save-the-Day, with a pink housecoat
wrapped around her like a cyclone and doobie
pins in her hair . . . and here I was, the dumb lil'
sidekick.

I couldn't believe this. I had a good mind to
beat-down my sister myself. I told her time and
time again she was going to get in trouble and to
stop staying out all night. I told her and I told
her . . . and what did she do? She did what she
wanted to do and now she's turned my mother
into a raving lunatic in matted bedroom shoes
flopping against the concrete.

"All I try and do . . ." my mother said as we
walked onto Qua's porch. "It's just never enough,
is it, Seven? Y'all just running around in the
streets buck wild like two lil' hooligans."

"Ma, I didn't do nothin'."

"Shut up, 'cause you were thinkin' somethin'
when I walked in that room. I swear, I try . . . and
I try . . . and I try . . . and I try . . ."

Oh God, she was repeating herself.

". . . And I try and what do I get in return? Children who lie to me and stay out all night!"

"I was in the bed. I come home every night!"

"Did I give you permission to talk?! Now, ring the bell!"

"Ma, we're right here," I said as we stood in front of the door. "Can't we just call her and tell her to come outside."

My mother pushed me on my shoulder. "Ring that bell." I hated that Toi's life had to end like this.

I rang the bell. "Who is it?" a deep voice yelled from behind.

"Qua, this is Seven. Is my sister there?"

"This not Qua, but hold up." A few seconds later the front door opened up and it seemed that the party from outside had drifted in here. The room was filled with Qua's boys, the TV was extremely loud and turned to ESPN, and Jay-Z and Beyoncé's "Bonnie and Clyde" was bumpin' through the Bose speakers. There was alcohol all about, with open bottles of Seagram's Seven gin and juice mix, Thug Passion, and passion fruit Alizé. And the air smelled like weed. "Wassup, Ma?" Qua said as he stood in the doorway.

"A whole lot gon' be up," my mother said as she stormed in, "if Toi Sharee McKnight . . . don't get her ass out here! Right now!"

"Yo," one of Qua's boys said, "I thought Shortie

said she ain't have no sisters." He looked my mother up and down. "I'm sayin', though, what's good with you boo. You easy like your sister in the other room?"

"Lil' boy, I will hurt you! Toi, get yo' grown ass out here right goddamit now!"

"Hold up," Qua said, "you can chill with all that—"

"Ma." Toi came stumbling out of Qua's bedroom with her clothes twisted every which way but the right way, holding her shoes in her hand.

She is so stupid.

"Get your things!" my mother said with tears streaming from her eyes, but with a stern voice that dared anybody to try her. Qua just stood there looking at my mother like she was crazy. "You know you ain't got to leave, right?" he said to Toi as if he were ghettohood defending Boom-Kiki's honor.

My sister looked at him filled with amazement. "What?"

"Get your things!" my mother said more as a warning than a statement. "And let's go, Toi."

"I *said,*" Qua stressed, "you ain't gotta go nowhere." His looks seemed to shoot straight through my mother. "You cool right where you are." Then he looked at Toi, "I told you, I love you, girl."

"Ma . . ." Toi cocked her neck and spoke as if she were liberated and was now going to flex on my mother, yet I could still hear nervousness in her voice. Now I knew for sure she superseded dumb. "I don't appreciate how you came up in here and I think you need to just—"

"Need to just what?" My mother lifted her bat in the air. "Whip yo' retarded azz? If you think I'm leaving here without you, you even dumber than I thought, 'cause by the time I get finished with you, you'll be molly-whopped all over this spot. Now try me! *You ain't got to go*," my mother screamed, mocking them sarcastically. "*And you don't appreciate* . . . What don't you appreciate, Toi?! Huh? I don't appreciate having to go through forty-eight hours, thirty-nine minutes, and seventeen seconds of labor with you!

"I don't appreciate you coloring on my white walls when you were five. I don't appreciate you peeing in the bed until you were ten and I had to clean your pissy behind. What you don't appreciate! I don't appreciate having to spend all my damn money on some lil' ungrateful child who grew up to be a tramp and now she thinks she can stand up in my face like she's a woman and tell me where she is and ain't going 'cause she's listening to some triflin' nothin' of a dope dealer who can't even hustle his way out a paper bag, let alone off Nye Avenue. No good—dirty dog—I wish you would stand up here and talk to me crazy 'cause I promise you, I will whip, wop, and bop yo' azz all over this floor!" She mushed Toi in the head. "Now, I said let's go!"

I was hoping Toi didn't flex anymore and really try to stay here with Qua, because from what I could see my mother was prepared to bury both of them at any moment.

"Don't hurt nobody in that housecoat, big mama, wit' yo' sexy self," some of Qua's boys said as my mother snatched Toi by her shoulder and practically pushed her out the door.

From inside, Qua's boys shouted after my mama: "Look at you, girl, it's your world, girl . . . Yo, son, I wanna see Mama in the daylight." Another one said, "Mom, Dukes, forget lil' shortie duwap, why don't you punish me . . . !" and on they went.

My mother shoved Toi in the backseat of the car, slammed the door, and we took off. "How could you do this to me?" Toi screamed. "How could you?" she screamed again.

"Don't scream no more." My mother looked at her in the rearview mirror. "Not up in here. I'm warning you, don't do it."

"YOU HAVE RUINED MY LIFE!!!!!"

I was convinced Toi had lost her mind.

My mother pulled the car over so fast I just knew I had whiplash. As the tires came to a screeching halt, all I could do was close my eyes and pray my sister survived. My mother threw the car in park, turned around backwards, got on her knees, reached behind the seat, and all I heard was WHAP, BAP, BOOM! Then my mother turned back around and looked at her nails. "You be lucky I didn't break one!" Then she lit a cigarette and looked in the rearview mirror before taking off.

I was too scared to look in the backseat for fear that my sister was dead, but when I heard her sniffling, like she was suppressing the urge to wail, I knew she'd survived the beat-down.

When we got home, Cousin Shake was laying on the couch in a too-tight smoking jacket and long johns, pretending to be asleep, but it was obvious he wasn't, especially since he kept peeking at Toi with one eye half open while laughing out the side of his lips like a hissing snake.

My mother looked at Toi and spoke calmly, "I'm not gon' let you work my nerves anymore than what they are—yo' daddy is on 'em enough. But let me inform you of this: I brought you into this world and I will gladly take you out. If you ever let another man, excuse me, another boy stand up in my face and even attempt to *ever* get you to disrespect me, I'ma beat the living crap outta you. 'Cause from where I stand, you seem to have forgotten who gave birth to who. I'm the mother and father up in this piece and the only other grown one is Cousin Shake. You just sixteen, and in my house that doesn't make you an adult. And don't think you gon' break bad and storm outta here like you running away, 'cause that ain't an option either. You gon' stay here and get it together like you have some sense. Period. And no, we ain't discussing this. There's no reasoning you can do with me, and before you say it,

I don't care to understand how you feel. We're not equals, so I'ma forewarn you not to break bad by getting up in my face! And the next time you yell at me, I'ma tear ya throat out! Now, you will leave that grown man alone, 'cause if I catch you with him, I'm calling the police on him and you can bet your bottom dollar on that!

"Now, what you gon' do is be in this house everyday after school. Don't ask me to go nowhere because the answer is no. Don't get on that phone, don't do nothing but go to school and come home. Do you understand me?!"

Silence.

"I said do you understand me?!"

More silence.

I think Toi's mind has left the building.

My mother walked up to her and stood directly in her face, my mother's head towering over Toi's just a little. "Do you understand me?!"

"Yes," she mumbled as her chest heaved up and down.

"That's what I thought, now give me that cell phone and go to your room." Toi handed her the phone and started walking away. "And don't slam no door you ain't pay for!" my mother yelled behind her.

I stood looking around the living room before I thought to move. "Uhmm, is it okay?"—I pointed to the doorway—"if . . . if I—"

"Just go!" my mother screamed, " 'cause you have worked my nerves, too!"

"Witcha grown self!" Cousin Shake yelled as I walked out the room.

I went in our bedroom and Toi was in her bed crying into her pillow. When I closed the door, she turned over and looked at the ceiling. "Why would she do that to me? Ever since Daddy left she's been a mad woman! I can't stand her!"

"You don't listen, Toi. I told you Mommy was gon' flip."

"I didn't think she would show up at his house," she sniffed. "And I can't believe you told her where he lived."

"Believe it. You must not know about Grier McKnight. I was not about to die up in here protecting you."

"Whatever, Seven."

"Don't take it out on me. 'Cause quite frankly, you played yourself. You slept on Mommy and then you hangin' with Quamir. He knows how old you are. He knows you're still in high school and he doesn't even care."

"Don't ever in your life talk about whether my man cares or not. You just mad because Josiah don't want yo' elephant behind!"

I cut the light back on because I had to see this for myself. "You have lost yo' rabbit-behind mind, talkin' to me crazy. Don't be mad with me because you can't be a jump-off in peace! I don't know who you think you talkin' to, but you gon' get up offa me, 'cause I know the real deal and I'll give you what Mommy didn't. Trust and believe you don't want it wit' me homegirl, for real-for real!"

"Whatever . . . that's my dude and I'm *not* leaving him alone. You just mad because you don't have a man and Mommy is mad because hers left!"

"Girl, let's blow this popsicle stick, 'cause you sound 'bout as stupid as they come. 'Cause if you think Quamir is any better than Daddy, you better think again. At least Daddy still takes care of us. What Quamir gon' do when he gets you knocked up? The same thing he did with his two other baby mamas . . . leave!"

"Whatever. I forgot you were a little girl."

"Yeah, whatever. I forgot you were grown." I flicked off the light and lay down to sleep.

6

You changed the game
I liked it thug style . . .

—CIARA, "THUG STYLE"

We were on lockdown, Cousin Shake was the warden, and the only one allowed in the yard or the movie room was Man-Man.

Although Toi didn't flat out say sorry, she apologized by going to Mi-Mi's, coming back and hooking up my hair with a part down the middle and two fish braids on the side. And here I was again, fly to death. All week Shae was sweatin' me, and when I finally told her that Toi did my hair, before I knew it she was over my house this morning with two packs of hair and a comb.

"Don't hate, boo." Shae smiled at me, while Beyoncé's "Kitty Kat" video played in the background and Toi was putting Ambro gel in Shae's hair. "I been waitin' all week. Plus, the game is tonight . . . and I'm 'bout to be funky-fresh and fly to death, heyyy!!!!" Shae laughed.

"Y'all so silly," Toi said as she gathered one side of Shae's hair to braid it. "But I gotta admit, y'all be throwin' it on. But of course, you're no Toi."

"Whatever." Me and Shae both laughed as the phone rang.

"Ballin'!" I answered on the first ring.

"Yo, Shawtie. What you know good, gurl?"

What the heck was . . . Melvin doing on my phone? "No, for real." I gave a sarcastic laugh. "How'd you get my phone number?" I placed my hand over the receiver and hit the mute button and said, "Yo' baby daddy on the phone."

"Who, Chris Brown?" She turned her head.

"No."

"Mike Jones?" Her eyes popped out.

"Mike Jones, ill! Heck no, it ain't Mike Jones."

She turned around in her seat. "I know you ain't got Rick Ross on the line."

"Rick Ross?" Toi frowned.

"Shut up." Shae laughed. "I like Rick Ross."

"I don't know what kinda taste you got."

"Shae, it's Melvin," I said as he went on and on in my ear.

Toi pulled her hair back and looked into her face. "I know you ain't feeling Big Country?"

All Shae could do was blush. "I think I love him."

Toi fell out laughing. "You have the worst taste in the world."

"Shut up."

"What is he sayin'?" Shae whispered as Toi began to braid her hair.

I secretly hit the speaker phone and pressed the mute button as Melvin went on, "Yo, Shawtie, I'm sayin' though, when we gon' get this poppin'? 'Cause for real, you startin' to get on my nerves a lil' bit. Smell me?"

"On his nerves. Oh, no, he didn't?!" Toi cracked up.

"Is he tryna play me?"

"I think he already did . . . oh, I'm in love." Shae was grinning from ear to ear. "Now stop playing and do the hook-up."

"And you sure Big Country is turning you on?" I asked for confirmation.

"I'm already calling myself Mrs. Big Country."

Toi placed her hand to Shae's forehead to check for a fever. "You're sick."

"Just do it." Shae hit me on the arm.

"Ai'ight. Calm down, and get yo'self together."

I took the mute button off. "Melvin—"

"Please don't beg and don't come to school tryna scream on me and please don't turn into a stalker, 'cause that won't change my mind."

"Ah un rudeness! No, you didn't."

"We can be friends though. You good people and er'thang, but it's like I'ma big fish and you just a squirrel tryna get a nut."

"What?"

"I'm tryin' not to hurt your feelings but I don't want a gurl who gon' be on the porch all her life."

"The porch?! You the one from down south!"

"Ask him if he likes somebody else," Shae whispered.

If Shae wasn't my girl, I promise you I woulda checked Melvin's chin fo' sho'. I took a deep breath. "So what you sayin', you feelin' somebody else?"

"Ain't that obvious, Shawtie? Y'all city chicks don't take hints. I hate to say it like this, but chicks are all over this." I could just imagine him rubbing his big sweaty hands all over his body. *Somebody shoot me.*

"What chicks?" I sighed.

"What you all sighing for?"

"Nothin' Melvin. Who likes you?"

"Ciara, Rihanna, Lil' Kim, Lil' Mama, and I got some ole birds, too."

"Old Birds?"

"Yeah, Oprah. She and Gayle King be all on me. I tell you I'm puttin' Stedman Graham and Cory Booker to sleep. Smell me?"

"What . . . are you . . . talking about?"

"Oh, I forgot you ain't know about me."

I hit the mute button and screamed, "Jesus!" I took the mute button off and spoke into the phone, "I mean, in school, Melvin!"

"Oh, well you know, ya lil' friend Ki-Ki kicked some slickness to me."

Ki-Ki? "What she say?" I asked.

"Asked me do I like pork chops and gravy."

"Pork chops and gravy?" *Yuck!*

"Yeah, she said she was gon' cook me some."

"And what you say?"

"Shawtie, skinny chicks can't cook. I looked at her and asked her was she crazy? I don't trust no skinny girl, all them bones she has done stabbed me."

I hated that I had to laugh. "And what she say?"

"She ain't say nothin', but Deeyah was standing there and she said I played myself."

"Maybe Deeyah was trying to get with you?"

"Shawtie, please. I'm not lookin' to turn a special ed hoochie into S.S.I. housewife."

"That was a good one, Melvin. So let's see, who else . . ." I stalled.

"Wassup with ya gurl, Shae?" he blurted out, like he'd been holding this question in.

"Oh, you diggin' Shae?"

"Yeah, somethin' like that. Now don't get to cryin' on me, Shawtie. I know I probably just hurt your feelings, but Big Country keeps it real."

I'm just gon' ignore that. "So you know Shae is my best friend in the whole world."

"Yeah, that's why I don't want you to start cryin', 'cause you just got played all the way to the left."

"You really think you just played me to the left?" *He is really feeling himself.*

"Girl, you so far on the left, you lost. But Big Country still got love for ya, girl. We just ain't meant to be. Smell me?"

I couldn't help it. I started laughing so loud I didn't know what to do with myself. "Yo, Shawtie, don't cry. It's cool."

That made me laugh even more. Shae and Toi were laughing so hard tears were pouring from their eyes.

"Shawtie," Melvin said, "what you rollin' all on the floor, Shawtie? Awl, Shawtie, don't get nothin' on yourself . . . Get off the floor, Shawtie. You gon' mess up ya hair. It's gon' be alright, we can still be friends. Awl, Big Country done broke ya heart."

I wiped the tears that came to my eyes from laughing so hard. "Okay"—I sniffed—"Big Country, it's cool. It's cool. So when you gon' kick it to Shae?"

"Tonight at the game. I'm 'bout to throw it on extra hard wit' Cornbread. I'm gon' come on so sweet, she might pee on herself. See, I was a lil' shy with you."

"Shy?"

"Yeah, I gotta lil' Michael Jackson syndrome, and I held back some, but when I saw Shae at lunch, eatin' that burger wit' gravy on it, and she sopped up the lil' gravy soup with the corner of the bread, I was like 'There she is, Big Country's soul mate.' Plus, she real fly, smell me?"

"Melvin, Shae likes guys a lil' calmer. Just step to her and put the Mac Daddy vibe down like 'Girl, you look so good you make me wanna sing yo' name in the rain—' "

"Shawtie, have you gon' crazy? No wonder you don't have a man."

"You dis'n me, Melvin?"

"Naw, just keepin' it real."

"So, you want Shae's number?"

"Yeah, hit Big Country wit' them digits."

"You got a pen?"

"I don't need a pen, I'm puttin' 'em in my cell phone."

So I gave him Shea's number.

"Cool," he said.

And before I could say bye, he'd hung up and Shae's cell phone was ringing.

"It's him." She hit me on the arm.

"Dang, he couldn't wait to dump me."

Shae's phone kept ringing. "You gon' answer the phone?" I asked.

"Nope, I'ma let it go to voice mail and then I'ma call back in about an hour. Make him sweat me a lil' bit."

"Oh, yeah, yeah, yeah, that's right—make 'im wait."

For about a half hour more, Toi put the finishing touches on Shae's hair and then we decided to go sit in the bedroom. I changed out of my pajamas and slipped on some jeans, a chocolate and powder pink hoodie with the Rocawear symbol all over it, and a pair of Chocolate Moose Pastrys.

"I need to see my man," Toi moaned. "God, I hate this." She pulled the curtain back and looked at the iron black bars Mommy put on our bedroom window.

"Well, you know Mommy's working double shift today at the phone company, and then she's on nights at New Jersey Transit, so she won't be home until real late."

"Yeah, but Cousin Shake be all extra wit' it. If I even look like I'm leaving the house, the first thing out his mouth is, 'Didn't yo' mother shut you down?'"

"So what you gon' do?" I asked.

She twisted her lips and looked at the wall as if she were deep in thought. "I got it."

"What?" Me and Shae said simultaneously.

"Look." She rummaged through my side of the closet and pulled out my Burger King uniform. "Let me get this."

"My uniform?"

"Yes, Seven, please. You gotta let me get this."

"Why? What, they rockin' B.K. uniforms now?" I was looking at her like she was crazy. "Why you wanna wear my uniform? That thing ain't cute."

"No." Her face was lit up like Christmas. "I'ma tell Cousin Shake I got a job and I start today. This way I can spend a few hours with my boo and be back home before Mommy gets here."

"And what if Mommy asks you about this job?"

"I'll just tell her I quit, that fast food wasn't my thing."

"She'll never believe that."

"Yes, she will. You gon' let me wear it or not?"

"Go 'head, but if you get caught, don't put my name in it."

"I'm not the snitch in the family." She rolled her eyes at me.

"Whatever," I said as me and Shae watched her get dressed.

Once Toi was done hooking herself up like she really had a job, I opened the door and Cousin Shake and Man-Man practically tripped over each other as the drinking glasses they had in their hands rolled across our bedroom floor. "You were listening at my door?"

"You opened that door," Cousin Shake said, "like you was 'bout to do something."

"I can't believe you were listening to my conversation."

"We weren't listening to your conversation," Cousin Shake insisted. "Man-Man said he heard something about Toi having a job, so I figured I needed to check this out, especially since Grier done kidnapped y'all lil' love life. Over there on Nye doing naked cartwheels in the middle of the street, actin' like you come from a pack of wild dogs. If I was ya mama, you wouldn't never come off punishment."

"Smell me?" Man-Man smirked.

"Nerd." I growled at Man-Man.

"'Least I ain't a dog, booty scratcher."

I wanted to smack him. "Whatever. I'm going outside," I said, slapping Man-Man in the back of his head.

"And I'm going to work."

"You go on to work then, baby," Cousin Shake said, extremely nice. "Who woulda ever thought that lil' Kim would come outta jail and get a job?"

Since October was still warm, everybody from around the way was outside. Music was blasting from all different directions and cuties were just about everywhere. Shae and I sat on my porch, watchin' the cars that rode by. "Yo, wasn't that Dollah?" Shae said to me. "On that motorcycle?"

"Girl, please. Do not mention him."

"Did you ever find out what was up with Dollah and Deeyah?"

"No, and who cares?" I said.

"I was curious."

"Well Deeyah knows Josiah and Dollah hate each other, so why would she even go there?" I know I was sounding like a hypocrite, but who cares?

"That's Deeyah. Anyway, did you hear about Tynasia?"

"Tynasia, Toi's friend Tynasia?" I asked.

"Yeah, they still girls?"

"As far as I know."

"So what happened?"

"I heard she's pregnant . . . and word is, that baby daddy be kicking her butt."

"Stop lying," Shae said, surprised. "I'd heard that but I didn't believe it."

"And you know Habiba, that used to go to Tech last year?"

"Well, she stole Hafisa, who went with Shabazz, her man. And guess what?"

"What?!"

"They both pregnant at the same time."

We both laughed.

"There ya go, girl." Shae wiped tears from her eyes and nodded her head toward Ki-Ki who was coming up the block.

"She ai'ight," I said, shielding my eyes from the sun.

"Yeah, she ai'ight, as long as she's by herself. Otherwise she's a follower."

"Wassup?" Ki-Ki asked as she stood in front of my porch. "I see y'all over here kickin' it. Y'all comin' to the game tonight?"

"And you know this," I answered.

"For real, I think Central gon' freak Newark Tech tonight."

"Girl, you gettin' high?" Shae said. "We gon' kill them."

"For real," I agreed.

"Yeah, maybe," she said as she played with her cell phone. "Especially since last year ya boy Josiah was stompin' everybody on the court."

"My boy . . . where you get that from?" I hoped she couldn't see me suppressing a blush.

"Come on, Seven." Ki-Ki twisted her lips while she put her phone away. "You can keep it funky with me. Would you remind her, Shae, that we girls?"

"You need to remind her of that"—Shae frowned—"I don't remember that well."

"Oh, my God, we were the Hottie posse way before Deeyah came along. We go back to nursery school. We straight-up girls, and though we don't hang like we used to, I still consider y'all to be my best friends."

Shae didn't seem to be buying it, but I was moved. Ki-Ki had no reason to lie. Deeyah wasn't around and maybe Ki-Ki was scared not to be Deeyah's friend, especially since Deeyah thought she could tell everybody, including Josiah, what to do. So what would make Ki-Ki any different?

"Besides," Ki-Ki went on, "as far as I'm concerned, she stole yo' man. You were the one feeling him first and she knew that."

Now that part was true. When we were in elementary school everybody knew Josiah was my boo, but when we got in high school the game changed and Deeyah moved up the ranks. "Yeah, I did kinda feel like she took him from me," I said.

I looked at Shae who rolled her eyes, like already I was talking too much. But Shae never gives anybody a chance—her circle is mad tight anyway.

"Exactly," Ki-Ki said. "I thought you felt that way . . . so why don't you step to him?"

"Well, don't say nothing"—I looked in her eyes for confirmation she could keep a secret—"but I was kinda diggin' him in the hallway the other week in school. Girl," I was cheesin', "I wanted to kiss him *sooooo* bad."

"Oh, my God." Ki-Ki laughed. "Why didn't you?"

"Because Deeyah came actin' all crazy."

"That was her man, what you expect?"

"I ain't push up on him, he pushed up on me."

"Oh, well . . . how did you control yourself?"

"I told you, the raving lunatic came on the scene. Otherwise, it woulda been on like popcorn."

"Dang, girl, I know you be dreaming about him."

"All day and night."

"Ill, get away from here!" Ki-Ki said out of nowhere.

"What are you talking about?" I asked as I turned my head toward the street and saw Shae's mother with the same clothes she had on the last time we saw her. She had crust around her mouth and was giving Shae a toothless grin. "You got two dollars?" she asked.

"No!" Ki-Ki went off. "Don't nobody have no two dollars, you crusty, dirty-lookin' bum, crackhead! Ain't nobody giving you two dollars so you can run and smoke it all up. Find a ho stroll, 'cause I know that's where you comin' from."

"Ai'ight, Ki-Ki, that's enough," I said, praying that Shae's mother didn't go off and could keep their relationship a secret.

Shae sat on my porch stunned. I wanted to cry for her, because I know she was beyond ashamed. Why would her mother keep doing this to her? I may have been without my dad, but I was thankful I still had my mother and she wasn't on drugs.

Shae's mother didn't say anything, she simply diverted her eyes from Shae's and walked away.

After a few minutes, Shae rose from the step.

"Yo, I gotta get going. I need to walk my little brothers to the Leaguers for karate."

"Ai'ight, Shae." I felt like walking behind her and telling her everything would be okay. I knew she needed a friend. "Call me later."

"I will, girl. Bye, Ki-Ki."

"Bye, Shae."

As we watched Shae cross the street to go home, I snapped at Ki-Ki. "Why did you do that?!"

"What?" She looked at me surprised. "It wasn't no one but a stupid fiend begging for money."

"No, it was Shae's real mother! I can't believe you did that!"

"What?" Ki-Ki looked at me surprised and I noticed she started playing with her cell phone again. "That wasn't Shae's mother. Don't her mother live in Texas or Tennessee or some place?"

"Shae's mother is a fiend and she's been one all her life! And I don't appreciate the way you were talking to her. You ain't have to say nothin'! Now Shae probably feels like trash. Listen"—I stood up—"I need to go check on my friend, and you need to roll!"

"My bad," Ki-Ki said with a sly smile as she walked away. "My bad."

I walked over to Shae's house and her father let me in. I knocked on her bedroom door before I walked into her room. She was lying on her bed crying.

"Shae." I paused, because for a moment I didn't know what to say. "She didn't know."

"Who, Ki-Ki or my mother? 'Cause no, Ki-Ki didn't know," she said. "But my mother, she knew and she keeps doing this!"

"Well Shae . . . she is your mother."

"No, Seven, you don't understand. I have given her so many chances to be in my life and every time she told me she was going to get clean or better yet stay clean, I was always so excited. And she always played me. And just when I was ready to introduce her to the world as my real mother so I could stop faking the funk, what does she do? She gets high again . . . Do you know I have eight brothers and sisters and she has done this to all of us. Yet, I'm always the one ready to give her another chance."

"What? I thought it was just you and your two brothers?"

"No, my brothers and I have the same mother and father and that's why we're together."

"What?" I was in shock. "I thought brothers and sisters lived together?"

"Seven, please. Be for real. I have two older sisters. One on drugs, the other one was adopted and doesn't want anything to do with us. My oldest brother's in jail and I got a younger sister that's in a foster home someplace. I don't know where she is. And really, the last I heard, my mother had a baby and left the baby in the hospital."

"Wow," was all I could say.

"Exactly, so I know what I'm talking about when I say I don't want anybody to know who she is. If people knew my mother was a fiend, I swear to you I would never come back outside or go to school again."

"Now, Shae," I said, while thinking that maybe talking up for her, by telling Ki-Ki about her mother, wasn't such a good thing. "How is anyone going to find out? And you know your daddy is not gon' let you stop coming to school. So, please. Plus what I'ma do if you don't come outside? You need to understand you can't battle your mother's drug addiction. She's the only one who can."

"Yeah." She sniffed, as she wiped her eyes. "You're right."

"Besides"—I laughed—"you know Big Country waitin' on you to call him back."

"Oh, I forgot about my husband."

I gave her a big hug. "Big Country tryna bag you, girl."

"Shut up." She playfully mushed me in my head. "And let's call him."

After calling Melvin and hearing that his new pet name for Shae was Cornbread, Shae grabbed her clothes and we went back to my house to get ready for the game, all while listening to Neyo's "Because Of You."

And for the next couple of hours, before it was time to get dressed for the game, we watched BET, chose what I was going to wear tonight, took my braids out, washed and flat-ironed my hair.

Ni-Ni Simone

Role-played about what she would say to Melvin and dreamed up a life for me and Josiah.

I couldn't believe it was raining at the same time we needed to leave for the game, and there was no way after being on lockdown all week I was missing this . . . and it didn't seem that catching the bus was an option.

"How we gon' blow this popsicle stick?" Shae asked. "Your mother's at work, my daddy's car is being fixed, and neither one of us have any men in our lives with cars . . . And you know the rain gon' flake up this gel in my hair and your flat-ironed 'do is a wrap."

"Word." I stood at my bedroom window with the curtain pulled back, watching buckets fall from the sky.

I turned around and looked at Shae who sat on my bed, leaning back on her elbows, looking at the ceiling. She was dressed in light blue wide-leg jeans, an Apple Bottoms tie-waist kimono top, and a fake tattoo of four adjoining hearts on her stomach.

I popped my lips together, which felt thick from the MAC clear lip gloss. "There's a half hour left to game time." I ran my hands over the signature Coach scarf around my head and pushed my oval shades on top. "And not going is not an option."

"Heck no, everybody and they mama's mama

gon' be there. How would it look if we don't show? Everybody gon' think we straight corny or some nonsense."

"Maybe we should just chance it," I said.

"And mess up our hair? No way."

"Yeah . . ." I dragged out. "You're right." I had to think of something, especially since I had on the perfect pair of bootylicious Rocawear jeans with the signature pockets on the back, my hot pink tee which read "Miss Info," and a braided belt wrapped around my waist.

"Wait a minute, Shae." A light bulb just went off in my head. "I know somebody with a car who'll give us a ride."

"Well, what you waiting on?" Shae hopped off the bed. "Let's go."

I just discovered why we call him Cousin Shake, because every time he walks he shakes.

It took me about five minutes of staring at Cousin Shake get ready for his date before I made up my mind that being at the game was worth the aggravation I knew he was about to put us through.

Shae pushed me on the shoulder. "Ask him."

"Cousin Shake . . ." I watched him admire himself in the full-length mirror in his bedroom. I knew he thought he was beyond sharp, as he kicked his feet out to check the fat laces in his L.A. Gears. This time though, as he studied his clothes, he didn't just have on Hammer pants, he had on an entire suit.

"Oh, you couldn't be talking to me, Fat Mama, because last night when I was watching TV and I asked you to help me dig out the corns on my toes, you told me you'd rather be dead ... so what could you be callin' me for? You don't care nothin' 'bout Cousin Shake."

"I love you, Cousin Shake." I thought I would vomit.

"You don't love me, you love my money." *I didn't know he had any dough.* "Now what you want?"

"I was wondering ... if you ... could—"

"Come on, girl, I got to go. I gotta fifty-year-old tender waitin' on me to take her to the Ma$e concert and we got front row seats."

"*Ma$e?*" Shae said. "Who goes to see Ma$e?"

I shot her the evil eye. "Can you take us to the basketball game at our school?" I asked.

"Take a who? I don't think I heard correctly," he said.

"Can you, please"—I sighed—"take us to the basketball game at our school?"

"You and who, Chicken?"

"Yes, Cousin Shake, me and Shae."

"Oh, y'all wanna go to the game?"

"Yes," we both said.

"Uhmmm hmmm, so y'all wanna ride in my B.M.Dub'ya? Ain't this 'bout a blip? I should tell you no, for being so fresh all the time. Look at ya, one lookin' like a chicken and the other one lookin' like a bear ... Y'all round here thinkin' Cousin Shake is a joke, like I'm something to laugh at. But I'll have you to know I'ma grown man dawg and I don't appreciate some of the things y'all do."

laugh at. But I'll have you to know I'ma grown man dawg and I don't appreciate some of the things y'all do."

"Sorry, Cousin Shake." I mustered up as much sincerity as I could.

"Yeah, you sorry alright, downright sorry and trifling! But you lucky I'ma Christmas—"

"It's Christian," I corrected him.

"You know what I mean, but I'ma forgive ya . . . this time . . . But the next time I ask you to dig out the hard part of my corns, I expect you and them toenail clippers to come marchin'. You understand, Fat Mama?"

"Yes, Cousin Shake."

"For tonight, it's 'Yes, M.C. Shake.'"

"M.C. Shake?"

"Either you wanna go or you don't."

We sighed. "Yes, M.C. Shake."

"That's what I thought." He slid his *Men in Black* shades on. "Now, make it do what it do . . . and let's go!"

I couldn't believe we sank this low and were willing to ride around Newark in Cousin Shake's black hearse, with its gold spinners, leopard bedsheets for seat covers, and red velvet dice hanging around the mirror in the front window.

As soon as we took off, I slid down in the seat. His car was popping wheelies until it got a steady flow and then it took off like a bat outta hell. And the sound of it was unbelievable: it sang its way over Clinton Avenue like a broken motorcycle racing through snow, and what made it worse was that the CD in his CD player was stuck on repeat, and all that belted out of his twenty-two-inch speakers that sat next to Shae in the backseat was Luda's "Shake Ya Money Maker." I swear I felt like crying.

"Cousin Shake," I said about a block before we reached the school, "you can let us off here. We'll walk the rest of the way."

"Didn't you ask me to drop you off at the school?"

"Yes."

"Well, that's what I'm gon' do. How I'ma explain to your mother that on my way to the Ma$e concert, I dropped you off on the corner? 'Lest that's what y'all really came out here to do, walk the street corner."

"Okay, Cousin Shake, but you don't have to pull up directly in front of the place! Dang!" I should've known he would do this. He pulled his hearse directly in front of the school with a crowd of kids standing around, some looking on in amazement and others just laughing.

As I pulled the lever to get out the door, Cousin Shake informed me that the door didn't open from the inside and the windows didn't roll down so we would have to do like everybody else and climb our "grown asses out the hatchback!"

"For real, Cousin Shake, this not ATL," Shae said.

"And we ain't the twins," I spat. "I can't be seen

climbing through no hearse's hatchback! It used to be dead bodies back there!"

"You a lie. Me and my woman ain't dead," Cousin Shake insisted.

My eyes popped wide open. The visual he'd just painted was about to send me crazy.

"Cousin Shake, please." Shae folded her hands over her eyes. "I don't need to see that."

"Chicken and Fat Mama," he said sternly, "y'all minds filled with nothing but filth. That's exactly why you shoulda stayed on South 14th Street 'steada comin' here to get ya scrub on. Now I got a lil' fifty-year-old tender I'm tryna see, so either you gon' climb out on ya own, or I'ma come and get ya. And if I getcha, I'm fling you into the street." He grabbed a belt laying on the floor of the hatchback. "Now, tell me what you came to do." He started swinging the belt like a lasso.

"We gettin' out," I said.

"Thought so."

"Dang!" Deeyah laughed her way to the car. "Y'all really wanted to come to the game, didn't you?" I wanted to smack her. I looked at Shae, who was behind me. "You better getcha, girl."

"Bet y'all ain't screamin' ballin' now," Yaanah said. "If I ain't feel sorry for you I would laugh."

"Y'all two gotta problem wit' my ride?" Cousin Shake looked at them like they were 'bout to catch a beat-down.

"Yeah, you just played yourself," Deeyah spat.

"Shut up, Deeyah!" I yelled.

"Don't even worry 'bout it, Fat Mama. Shake got this." Cousin Shake looked at Deeyah: "Who mo' played out then yo' grandmama, with a mouth fulla chipped gold teeth, down there at the senior citizen home, talkin' 'bout she reppin' for hoochie life."

"You don't even know my grandmother!" Deeyah screamed.

"Yes, I do. All the freaks come out at night. Gon' call Shake played out. Who mo' played out than you in all them leg warmers, lookin' like rainbow-colored pigeon shit. Don't play with me lil' girl, 'cause I will turn yo' fresh behind upside down. Now unless you wanna be put over my knee, you'll skeet yo' lil' cockeyed self on outta here!"

Deeyah looked as if she wanted to cry. She rolled her eyes and she and Yaanah headed on inside.

"That's what I thought!" Cousin Shake yelled behind her. "You don't want none of this!" Cousin Shake looked at me and Shae. "Come on, Chicken and Fat Mama, be about it now. Let's go."

7

This is why I'm Hot
I'm Hot cause I'm fly . . .

—MIMS, "This Is Why I'm Hot"

The music was bumpin' as the spotlights shot back and forth across the court like a disco ball twirling over the dance floor. Clouds of fake smoke filled the air as the players made their grand entrance to kick off the season. Everybody who was anybody was here, making the gymnasium mad crowded, leaving us with practically nowhere to sit. The bleacher's top rows were already filled and since we were late we had no choice but to sit on the bottom row, directly off the court, and next to some chick who must've been chewing her whole pack of gum at one time.

"Could you . . ."—I tried to be as nice as possible—"kinda slow up with poppin' the gum . . . Thank you."

"Oh, my fault, boo"—and that's when I realized she was somebody's mama—"wit' yo' cute self."

She smiled at me. "Look at them dimples. Girl, when I was yo' age, Lawd have mercy, I was 'bout yo' size and I was straight killin' 'em all. Lawd knows they had two words for me: Brick house!"

Me and Shae fell out laughing. This lady was trippin'. She had a fly short haircut with spikes at the top and blonde streaks running through it. She wore a pair of jeans and a shirt that read "Josiah's mama" in rhinestones. Josiah's mama . . . oh . . . my . . . God.

"Shae." I tugged on her arm and pointed to the woman's shirt.

"Oh, that's a hot ghetto mess!" Shae laughed. "That's your future mother-in-law. You gon' have Josiah's name in rhinestones on your shirt, too. Now be quiet and let's hear the players be introduced."

Honestly, the only player I remember being introduced was God's gift to me: number twenty-three, better known as Mr. Six-foot-two, one hundred seventy pounds, athletically built Josiah Whitaker. He walked on the court so smooth that I promise you all the air had floated out of me and was swept under his feet, which is why I kept striving to breathe.

"If you don't calm down," Shae said to me, "you gon' hyperventilate."

"Girl, you don't understand, look at him—"

"I'm lookin', but I still don't see what you see, 'cause he way too scronie lookin' for me. The lil' daddies I like got to have some meat on 'em."

"I forgot you were reppin' for the big boys."

"All day long, home slice. You better recognize. Now, especially since his Proactiv worked, Melvin can get it any day of the week."

"I'm 'bout to throw up. Let's just watch the game."

The two centers, one from each team, stood in the middle of the court for jump ball to start the game. Everybody was hooping and hollering, "Work it out, Tech!" as our team snatched the ball. Already we were killing it.

I really tried to concentrate on the game, but Josiah's calf muscles floated up and down in his beautiful brown legs and the flexing of his biceps and triceps was 'bout to send ya girl crazy. Jesus . . . Jesus . . . Jesus . . . was all I could say.

As the coach called a time-out, Shae leaned against my shoulder and whispered, "Three o'-clock."

When I turned to my right, Deeyah was standing in the corner with Dollah. He was whispering something in Deeyah's ear and then she whispered something back in his and massaged his goatee, and then he ran back to the bench, where his coach looked to be scolding him.

"I can't believe," I said to Shae, "that Deeyah was all hugged up on Dollah like Josiah was invisible. I don't believe this."

"Told you she was a ho. You better do the damn thing and step to Josiah. She don't appreciate him."

And that was true, she didn't appreciate him. How could she have spazzed out when she saw us in the hall, but be hugged up in the corner with ole boy, just kickin' it like it's nothing.

I looked at Ki-Ki who was sitting behind me. "What's crackin' witcha girl?"

"What you care?" Ki-Ki smirked. "That you right there." She pointed to the court and said, "Handle that."

I looked back at the court and Josiah was staring at me the same way he was looking at me when he was at my job. After staring at me he looked at Deeyah. I guess he was trying to get his focus back on the game, because when his teammate threw him the ball, he took a shot and missed.

"That's alright, baby!" his mother shouted, while clapping her hands. "Don't even worry 'bout it!"

I couldn't help but wonder if she was talking about Deeyah or the game.

After missing his shot, Josiah tossed the ball to one of the other players, but one of the guys from the opposing team caught it and made a two-point play. I hated that Deeyah was messing up his game. But after a few missed shots, Josiah was back on top and ruling the court. His mother was standing on her feet and kept shouting, "That's my baby! Do that, baby! Whip 'em, baby! And whip 'em real good!"

At halftime everybody was kickin' it.

"Ballin' . . . !" Deeyah said to me, smiling and poppin' gum, with Ki-Ki and Yaanah standing beside her. "I'ma forgive yo' great grandfather for what he said to me."

"Whatever." I blew her off.

"See, and I was coming to give you a compliment," she said.

"Why are you being nice to me?"

" 'Cause you look too cute for them to be plus-size clothes, just like a round lil' chubby ho." She laughed. "That's why Josiah was wasting his time talking to you in the hall the other day, 'cause he know round chubby hos don't get no play."

"Excuse me." Josiah's mother looked at Deeyah and rolled her eyes. "You wanna show some respect?"

"Ill, and who are you?" Deeyah snapped. "Hmph, I don't remember you being my mama."

I could tell that Josiah's mother was 'bout to give Deeyah the business and I was 'bout to take pleasure in this.

"You're right, I'm not your mama because if I was, you would have some respect and if you know like I know you'll take your voice down, Miss."

Deeyah cocked her neck to the side and that was my clue to jump in, 'cause it was obvious these two didn't know each other. "Excuse me." I smiled. "Mrs. Whitaker, is it?"

"Yes."

"Well, Mrs. Whitaker, this is Deeyah, Josiah's girlfriend . . . and Deeyah, this is Mrs. Whitaker, Josiah's mother."

"Oh honey, please." Josiah's mother rolled her eyes. "No wonder he ain't never brought you to the house, 'cause he was raised better than to have a has-been in my living room." She sucked her teeth. "Now." She turned to me. "Sweetie, watch my bag, please. I'm going to the bathroom."

"Dang, Deeyah"—I laughed—"I guess it's official. You really are a has-been."

"And I guess you really are chubby."

"Is that all you can say?" I snapped. "Why you don't think of another comeback?"

"Yeah," Shae said, " 'cause on the real she shaped better than yo' boxed-up behind."

"Why don't you mind your own b.i.?" Deeyah spat at Shae.

"How Seven know his mother and you don't?" Ki-Ki asked Deeyah, like she had an attitude.

"Why you worried about it?!" Deeyah opened her eyes wide and looked at Ki-Ki.

" 'Cause you're the one who said you be at his house every weekend and that his mother loved you."

"Okay, I gotta question for y'all." She pointed at all of us. It was obvious that Deeyah didn't appreciate being put on blast. "Why you trippin' through my business so hard? You need to be worried about your own boyfriends. Oops, I forgot you don't have any. Now I'm going to get some soda." And she walked away.

"That's y'all girl." Shae sat back down on the bleachers. " 'Cause RaShaeyah is not beat."

"Yeah whatever . . ." Ki-Ki gave a sinister smile. "She got mo' friends than you." And she and Yaanah walked away.

"What does that mean?" I asked Shae.

"Who cares?" Shae rolled her eyes. "Told you she a raggedy mess anyway."

Before I could respond, the game was about to start again and everybody returned to their seats.

Tech was killing it and everybody knew it. It was official by the time the game ended—we had the baddest team in all of Newark.

"Yo, Cornbread!" Melvin yelled toward us as everybody started making their way to leave. "Let me hollah at you for a minute."

He walked over to Shae and placed his arm around her. "Don't hate, Shawtie." He looked at me. "You had your chance. Now go wait outside, she comin'."

Oh no, he didn't?! "Oh, ah un rudeness! Don't do it to yourself, Melvin," I said.

"How you gon' tell my best friend to stand outside in the rain? And just when I thought you were cute," Shae said.

"Shawtie know Big Country was just playin'. Matter-fact, I'ma give y'all a ride. So can we please get a few minutes?" he said to me. "Alone."

"I'ma wait in the hall, Shae." I rolled my eyes at Melvin.

"Ai'ight." She said with a pint-sized grin on her face.

SHORTIE LIKE MINE

When I stepped in the hall I overheard Josiah tell Deeyah, "Ma, just go 'head." I stepped back and stood still so they couldn't see me. People were passing by, but no one but me seemed to pay them any mind.

"I told you before," he went on, "this was a wrap. I'm not feeling you no more. Plus you was all up on Dollah and I already warned you about him."

"Oh, like you weren't in the hall with Ms. Big-Behind Seven."

"So if I was, maybe that's what I like."

That's right girl, I wiggled my neck, *a big behind is what he likes. Now take yo' anorexic self outta here! Bye-bye, heifer!*

"It's really none of your concern," he continued, "so chill, be as grown as you say you are, and step."

"Oh, it's like that?!" Deeyah spat at Josiah.

He sighed. "What you ain't, you know."

"You just played yourself."

"Yeah and I'm shook." He smirked. Before he could go on, Dollah walked up with a towel thrown around the back of his neck and a duffel bag on his shoulder. He still had on the team's red and white basketball uniform. As he walked by he grabbed Deeyah's index finger and pulled it just enough so she would step away from Josiah a little. When she turned her head he said, "I see you, ma." Then he looked at Josiah and winked his eye.

"Is there a problem, son?" Josiah spat.

"Not unless you wanna make it one." Dollah stopped dead in his tracks. "You need to put all that thug in ya game."

"You need to get a game." Josiah stepped to the side. "Like I told you before, it's whatever, Chief."

"You threatening me?"

Don't ask me what went through my mind when I decided to play superwoman, but there was no way I was gon' let some broke-down Snoop get with my man, so I walked up and said, "You better fall back, 50 Cent—"

"Ill." Deeyah rolled her eyes. "Where did you come from? Off a diet?"

"Excuse you, Superhead?"

Josiah looked at me and smiled. "I knew it was a reason I liked you." He winked his eye and waved his hand. "Forget them." He brushed Dollah slightly on the shoulder as he passed him to step my way. "You cute, you know that?"—he placed his arm around my neck—"all defending my honor."

"Don't gas yourself." I was doing my all not to blush.

"I don't have to." He smiled. "You already did."

"Yeah, ai'ight," I said as we started walking down the hall.

"You know you shouldn't have called that girl Superhead." He laughed. "You wrong for that."

"See, and I was about to give you props for having a good game."

"And we know this." He stroked my cheek.

"And who gave you permission to touch me?"

He laughed. "So wassup, lil' mama?" He looked me up and down. "Look at you, tryna get yo' grown and sexy on."

"Uhmmm, pretty much." I hoped he couldn't tell I was nervous, but at any moment I was due to break.

"How you get here, you need a ride?"

"Uhmmm." I had to think for a minute if I should ride with Big Country or fulfill my destiny. I smiled at Josiah. "Yeah, I need a ride."

"Come chill wit' me, then."

"I'll meet you outside." I walked back into the gym and over to Shae, with my heart racing a thousand miles per minute. "I got a ride, so you and Big Country can handle that." She didn't seem too disappointed with his arm draped around her.

"Okay, Seven, no problem." I don't even think she looked my way when she said that.

Josiah drove a silver '89 Acura Legend. His car may have been old but it was fly, kitted up, and fully loaded. When I sat down in his black leather passenger seat I felt as if I belonged there and all that had been missing from his car was me. He turned on the radio and Ciara's "And I" was playing . . . which I swore had to be our song. Oh, I was in love and he just didn't know it.

I couldn't believe this was happening to me.

This had only happened once before but I was dreaming, and my mother woke me up.

I pinched myself to see if this was real and so far it was . . . I was alive and the man sitting next to me was Josiah . . . I think there really is a God.

I psyched myself up to remain calm. I kept saying, *Seven, you got this. Just suck ya stomach in and be cool. Don't sweat it, 'cause you gon' mess up if you do, but you fabulous, remember that. Act like you would if Shae was around, just don't be as silly with it. Be sweet . . . like a Jolly Rancher.*

"Seven"—he looked at me and then quickly turned back to the street—"keep it funky. Why every time you around me, you ain't pushin' up? You see I'm here, what more ya man need to do? You see I'm tryna get wit' you."

I almost had whiplash, my heart was thundering so loud I thought we had an accident. I was tempted to ask him to check my pulse. "What are you talking about?"

"Like for instance, the other day at your job, you didn't even say nothin'."

"Boy pa'leese, you played me so far to the left I was on the right."

Josiah fell out laughing. "Yo, that's the end of that. You killing me with the jokes. Besides, it was you . . ." We stopped at a red light. "You leave me speechless." He cocked his head to the side and stared at me.

I didn't know what to say, so I said, "Why you and Dollah always beefin'?"

"Dollah? You wanna talk about Dollah?" I could tell he was caught off-guard.

"I just asked a question." I felt like I was defending myself.

"Ai'ight, me and Dollah always beefin' because he don't have no respect."

"I don't think Deeyah would agree."

"How about this—any chick that messes with Dollah is a ho. Period."

"A ho?" I took offense. I started to place my hand on my hip and say, *"Listen, baby daddy, don't be calling me no ho, ya scrub!"* But instead I said, "Well, if Deeyah is a ho because she messed with Dollah and you messed with Deeyah then what does that make you?" *Let's see how you come back from that one, Mr. Judgmental.*

"It makes me available."

Oh, I love him so much!

"Besides," he went on, "all Dollah gon' do for Deeyah is supersize her meal at Burger King." He took off as the light turned green.

"No, you didn't dis Burger King."

"You know what I mean. And listen, the next time you don't know how to respond to something I just said to you, don't change the subject. Just look at me and tell me how you feel or better yet, just admit you don't know what to say."

I tucked my bottom lip into my mouth and for

a brief moment I didn't feel sixteen. I felt grown and for some reason I felt uncomfortable about it.

I guess he could tell that I was feeling funny, so he laughed and said, "So what, you like all the other chicks? You on me 'cause I play ball?"

"Ah un rudeness." I gave him a talk-to-the-hand motion. "If I'm not mistaken, you tryna kick it to me. Besides"—I clicked my tongue—"do I look like a groupie?"

"Turn to the side and let me see. Yeah, you look a lil' like a groupie, right around the nose."

I punched him playfully on the arm. He stopped at another red light. "What?" He smiled. "You mad?"

I pouted my lips and my dimples sunk like a ship's anchor into my cheeks. I gave him the same look I used to give my daddy when I wanted my way.

"Oh, now you wanna give me that look."

"What look?" I held the magical face.

"The look that made me notice you in the first place. The look that's gon' end up letting you get your way."

"I don't know what you talking about."

The light changed. "Sure you don't. And stop looking at me like that before I start acting stupid, carrying your books and doing your homework everyday." He laughed.

And I laughed too. But little did he know I was

tucking my "get what I want" look in my back pocket, in case of an emergency.

Before I knew it we were in front of my house. He cut the car off and turned to look at me. "So, tell me what you need."

"Somebody that's down for me." *I know I sound stupid*.

"Yeah, I got you, ma." He brushed my hair behind my ear and faced me. "Man"—he paused—"you so pretty."

I hated that I couldn't stop blushing.

"So I was thinking"—his left arm hung over the steering wheel and his right arm draped around my shoulder—"that maybe we could do this." And just as I closed my eyes and felt his lips press against mine, I heard my mother calling my name. Instantly I jumped and turned around. I thought I was dreaming again, but this was real and my mother was standing at his car window in tears.

"Ma." I jumped out the car. "I'm still a virgin."

"Seven—"

"And that was my first kiss . . ."

"Seven—"

"Matter-fact, it wasn't even that good."

"Would you shut up?!"

I felt like the world's biggest dummy. "What's wrong?"

"I need you to stay in the house with Man-Man. I need to go pick up your sister."

"Where is she?" I panicked.

"In jail." My mother looked around like she

was lost. "I gotta go, Seven!" and she jumped in her car and left.

"Do you need me, Seven?" Josiah said, before I turned and went in the house. As I shut the door and tears filled my eyes, I couldn't quite remember if I'd said good-bye.

8

All I need in this life of sin
Is me and my boyfriend . . .

—JAY-Z FEAT. BEYONCÉ, " '03 BONNIE & CLYDE"

It was six o'clock in the morning and I had to sit through my mother screaming and crying about how tired she was of *us* not listening. Here was the *us* again, and I hadn't done anything. Apparently Ghetto Charming, better known as Quamir Davis, had a number assigned to his name that was plastered across his Essex County Jail ID. One that my sister must've been fond of, because now she had one of her own, except hers was from Essex County Juvenile Detention Center.

According to the *Star-Ledger*, Quamir's house was a drug trap, and you know who was laid up in the bed when the place was raided. And although she was under eighteen, they arrested her, took her to juvie, and released her to my mother's custody, which all added up to this: Toi hadn't learned her lesson so my daddy had left Hollywood and returned to Ghettowood so he could stand in my mother's kitchen in the same spot where he told her he was leaving us, with his chest puffed out, giving us a look like he could still tell us what to do.

"You know not to say nothing to me, right?" I spat at Toi after my mother instructed me to get up from the table and get ready for school. Toi just sat there with tears streaming down her copper cheeks, wearing my Burger King uniform that I'd completely forgotten she had on. "Stupid."

"That's enough, Seven!" my mother interjected, "'cause you're not exactly off the hook, either. Don't think I didn't peep that your sister had on your work uniform, which means she snuck out with your assistance. So actually I should get you for not minding your business and interfering with me raising my child. I have reasons for the things I do and I don't appreciate you all breaking my rules, like you grown. And if the truth be told, the only reason I haven't caught either one of y'all"—she waived her index finger—"with a one and two is because if I do, I'm really hurt you, so it's best if I keep my hands to myself . . . at least at this moment . . . but oooh hoooooo." She smirked. "Y'all will get it, trust me. Be on notice and at all times, when you around me, watch ya back, 'cause I'm comin' for you!"

"Witcha grown self!" Cousin Shake threw his two cents in. "Lyin' to me like lil' Kim had a job."

"Oh, she had a job," my daddy added, "a job working for Quamir, the kingpin!" All I could do was roll my eyes at the top of my head. My daddy thinks every drug dealer is a kingpin. Well, if that's the case, I should think that every light skinned black man who looks like Boris Kojo—just like my daddy does—is a no good dirty dog, who cheats on his wife and trades his old children in for a new one. "I didn't raise you to be with no kingpin!" he spat.

"He wasn't a kingpin," my sister cried. "You need to mind your business!"

"Yeah, what you care for?" I added. "Don't you have another family to be concerned about? What you here for anyway? To show off your new life?!"

"Don't speak to your father like that!" my mother defended him.

"Who the hell are you two talking to?!" My daddy raised his voice as the veins in his neck thumped. "I'm your father!"

"And when did you think of that, before or after you left us?" I asked.

"I didn't leave you! I left your mother! There's a difference."

"There's no difference. That's my mother and what you did to her you did to all of us. So you can just go back to where you came from. And don't think you came back here to sleep in my mother's bed!"

My daddy's eyes bugged out but as he stormed

toward me, Cousin Shake stood in the way. "Calm down, Tre. She's a good kid. She's just hurt that's all."

I did all I could not to cry. "I gotta get ready for school."

I looked at my sister and rolled my eyes. "All this behind a dang weed pusher!"

"Oh, so that's what he was!" my mother snapped. "A weed pusher. You proud of yourself, Toi? You've ruined your life behind some low-level weed pusher, so now what kinda life you gon' have for your baby?!"

"Baby, what baby?" I spun around toward my sister and asked.

"Tell her!" My mother screamed with tears flying from her eyes.

"Calm down, Grier," my daddy said.

"Don't you," she spat at him as if there were a knife in her throat, "say nothin' to me . . . I could take and smack the hell outta you right now, you know that?! The answer to your question, Seven, is that your sister's pregnant!"

Immediately my mouth flew open and Cousin Shake started living up to his name and shaking all over the place. Did my mother just say that my sister was pregnant? Oh . . . my . . . God, this must be somebody else's life. Tell me that she did not go out and get knocked up by Quamir. She must've been born dumb because there is no way you just stumble upon this type of stupidity.

"You're pregnant, Toi?" I was in shock. Of all

the things I knew she could be, being pregnant wasn't one of them. "Huh? How do you know that?"

"Answer your sister!" my mother screamed.

"I've known all week. I just didn't tell nobody but Qua."

"What you gon' do with a baby?"

"Don't you worry about what I'ma do with my baby!" Toi yelled. "My child is wanted, me and Quamir wanted a family."

I didn't think my mother's hand could travel so fast as it did across Toi's cheek. "You not even eighteen and you planning to have a family? Are you serious? Do you know what being pregnant means! You grown now, you know that, right? I had three kids and I'm only taking care of three I had. Anybody else that comes in here is on their own."

"And I'm on disability so don't even look at me," Cousin Shake added.

"She's getting an abortion," my daddy said matter-factly. "There's no way she's having a baby by some lowlife, who's just going to leave her to raise this child alone. My daughter will not have that kind of life!"

"No," my mother said. "That's reserved strictly for her mother."

My father looked at her and immediately shut up.

"I'm having my baby," Toi cried.

"So now you're ready to be a mother?" I could see my mother's broken heart written all over her face. "And what's your plan, Toi, have you worked that out? So you gon' work, go to school, raise a baby, pay for a sitter, take this child to the doctor, and somehow in between all of this be a teenager?! What about college, Toi? What about making something of yourself?! You wanna be like me, working two jobs to make ends meet?! Is this where you wanna be the rest of your life? I swear, you're a bigger fool than I thought."

"It's not your problem," Toi snapped at my mother. "So what you worried for?! You too busy working all the time and running from daddy, dogging you out. You just bitter, a bitter, jealous, and nagging woman who could only dream up how to keep a man, so don't you worry about me. Me and my man, we got this!"

Before anyone knew it, my mother had slapped Toi so hard she fell backwards out of her chair. "I don't know who you think you talking to"—she hovered over Toi—"but let me tell you something. Don't you ever, and I mean ever as long as you stay black and there is a God, ever speak to me like that again, because as sure as I'm standing here, you gon' die. Let me tell you something, little girl. I'ma woman and I can take care of me and mine. What can you take care of? In case you forgot, I take care of you. Who do you think pays the light bill, the phone bills, the gas bill, the mortgage, buys food, cooks the damn food, buys clothes, and everything else you need? Me, the nagging, bitter, and jealous one! My mother always told me that two women can't live in the same house so since you so grown, you need to figure out where you gon' go. You going back to California with your father?"

"I—I—I—I—" my father stuttered.

"That's what I thought. So it looks to me, Miss Toi, that since your boyfriend's in jail and your daddy don't seem to want you where he is, you homeless. Which means you don't have a rusted pot to piss in or a cracked window to throw it out of!"

"Grier, you being a little too hard on the girl," my father said. "She's getting an abortion period and that's the end of it."

"You can't make her have an abortion, Tre!"

"I'm having my baby," Toi repeated, sounding sure of herself.

"And how are you going to do that?" my father asked.

"My child has a father! Besides, we're getting married!"

"I'll be damned. You're under eighteen and there's no way I'm signing you over to some king-pin named Qua."

"You gon' get married when?" my mother asked. "Before or after he gets outta jail, or better yet, before or after you do? You got a case remember, and when we left the precinct this morning he still hadn't claimed the drugs as his own, which means you're more than parents, you're codefendants on a case."

"Grier, don't tell the girl that," my father said. "I'ma get you a lawyer and pray that he can make this go away."

"Why are you always looking for something to go away?!" my mother screamed at him. "Is that why you left us here and moved to the other side of the country? Because you wanted us to go away so you could play Daddy-of-the-year to your kid over there!"

"Now wait a minute, I never gave up on my kids. I call here and nobody wants to talk to me. What am I supposed to do?!"

"All I know is that this is a mess! A complete and utter mess! Go to your room!" my mother screamed at Toi. "I'm sick of looking at you! And Seven, what did I tell you to do? I said get ready for school!"

This had to be a nightmare. I simply left the kitchen, got dressed for school, and met Shae at the bus stop.

"Why you so quiet?" Shae asked as we rode the bus.

"My sister's pregnant." I sighed.

"What?" Shae said as if I'd spoken a foreign language.

"You heard me, she's pregnant. And that's not the whole of it."

"What else?"

I pressed the buzzer so we could get off at the upcoming stop. "She got arrested last night. Qua's house was raided and she was there when it happened."

"You lyin'."

"No, I'm not lyin'," I said as we stepped off the bus. "She's just stupid."

All morning during class I had a bad feeling in my stomach, like my whole life was coming to an end. I chalked it up to me being too close to my sister and maybe feeling some of her pain . . . or me being ticked about how dumb she'd turned out to be. But whatever the reason, I wished this feeling would go away.

Finally it was lunchtime and I could sit down and talk to Shae about how I was feeling, about Josiah, and everything that happened last night. And of course I couldn't wait to hear what action she and Melvin had gotten into.

When I went to the cafeteria, Shae, Yaanah, Ki-Ki, and Deeyah were all sitting at a table together. From the look on Shae's face, this was not her idea.

"Yo, Cornbread!" Melvin yelled as I walked to the table and sat next to Shae. He sat a tray of food in front of her and said, "That's for my boo."

Heck. I looked around for Josiah, who was sitting at a table with his boys gettin' a serious grub on. Dang, for a quick minute I was hatin'. "Look at you." I smiled at Shae who was glowing.

"Wow," Ki-Ki said, "look at you, Shae. And to think I've been feeling sorry for you."

"Sorry for me?" Shae frowned. "For what?"

"Uhmmm, nothing . . . at least not yet."

"So, Seven," Deeyah snapped, cutting across Ki-Ki, "no need to lie. You tryna get with Josiah? You know he don't like fat girls. He only gon' use you to do his work and get straight As."

"And what he use you for?" I snapped. "'Cause it sure wasn't your grades."

"You're a miserable slob," Deeyah said that so loud that the entire cafeteria became quiet. "And word is that you a ho, 'cause you don't even know Josiah and already you sleeping with him. And I won't mention what else you doing that's hittin' below the belt!"

"Oh, heck no!" Shae jumped up. "What you wanna throw Deeyah?! 'Cause you ain't 'bout to be talking to my girl like that!"

"Your girl. Oh, please!" Deeyah snapped. "Play it, Ki-Ki." And at that moment Ki-Ki whipped out her cell phone and played my entire conversation about me being in love with Josiah and wanting him for myself, and me not caring that he was Deeyah's boyfriend. I couldn't believe this. She had recorded our conversation? Is that why she kept playing with her cell phone that day? Oh . . . my . . . God . . . I don't believe this. I had never been so humiliated in my life. Everybody, including Josiah, was looking at me like I was crazy.

"Excuse you," Shae snapped, "but I know y'all skeezin'—sleezin'—skanky—havin' crab—coochie infected—boostin' behinds—are *not* tryna scream on my girl?! 'Cause I really don't know what you showin' off for. Everybody knows you've slept with every Tom, Dick, and Raheem in here. Excuse you, but please remind me, Seven, of who got suspended last year for being caught in the janitor's closet with Khalil?"

"Ki-Ki."

"Thank you. And who was pregnant by Sef at the same time that Yaanah was going with him, huh?"

"Deeyah."

"And what happened to that baby?"

"Let's just say she had to pray for forgiveness."

"And for an extra added bonus"—Shae sucked her teeth and pointed at Yaanah—"in case you even thinkin' about gettin' involved, Seven, please tell me who is still a virgin but tryna her best not to keep it funky?"

"Yaanah."

"Oh, y'all trippin' real hard!" Ki-Ki said in disbelief. "Okay, well how about this: 'least my mother ain't a beggin' fiend on the street." She looked at Shae.

"My mother's a nurse in Tennessee. She's nobody's fiend and she don't beg on the street."

"Well, if it's a lie then, ya girl, that you was just shootin' all that ra-ra over, told it." And as if on cue, Ki-Ki's phone continued to play the rest of our conversation . . . *Shae's mother begs on the street. She's been a fiend all her life . . .*

SHORTIE LIKE MINE

Shae looked at me with tears in her eyes. "You told her that?"

"She told everybody that. She's always talking about you," Deeyah lied. "We've always known, we just felt sorry for you, 'cause we all knew that your daddy doubled as your mommy!"

I could tell that Shae wanted to cry. "She's lying! Stop lying!" I shouted at Deeyah. I reached over the table to Ki-Ki, who backed away: "Tell the truth!" I looked back at Shae and said, "I was talking up for you that day. That was on Sunday when Ki-Ki was sitting on my porch . . . and you know what happened. I was protecting you. I would never talk about you. You gotta believe me."

"Don't ever"—Shae's bottom lip trembled—"say nothing to me. You were supposed to be my best friend and this is what you do? I swear to God, I hate you!" And she ran out the cafeteria.

Everybody was looking at me and I felt worse than a gutter rat. "That's messed up, Shawtie," Melvin said to me as he left to find Shae. "Yo, Cornbread, hol' up."

Suddenly all I could see was red. I reached for Ki-Ki, grabbed her by the collar, and with all my might dragged her over the lunch table. But before I could wham on her, Josiah pulled me off her and stood between us. "Go sit down!" he said sternly to Ki-Ki.

"Bring it!" Ki-Ki kept screaming. "Bring it! No, don't hold me back!" she spat at some of our other classmates who held her back by her arms.

The entire cafeteria was in an uproar and it was only a matter of moments before the principal would be in here telling us he was calling our parents and sending us home.

"No, you bring it Ki-Ki. You comin' for my throat and I didn't even do nothing to you! Please step to me so I can teach you a lesson or two!"

"Yo, what I say? Calm down!" Josiah said to me. "You gon' blow your honors status and everything you worked for in school for some jealous little chicken-head. Forget her!" Then he turned to Deeyah. "And you, it's mighty funny how you tryna rag on Seven when you were just in my face a minute ago tryna give it up to me in the hallway, even though I told you then it was all about her and I wasn't feeling you no more!"

"You a chicken-head, Josiah!" Ki-Ki screamed.

He didn't respond. Instead he kept telling me to calm down but that's when I started crying and stormed out. By the time I got to my locker to collect my things, Josiah was behind me. "Where you going?" he asked.

"I'm leaving."

"Why?"

"Because I gotta find Shae and I just saw her run out the door. I need her to understand that it wasn't like that! I would never do that!" Tears were flowing down my face like rain. "That's my best friend. I love her like my sister, Josiah. You don't understand."

SHORTIE LIKE MINE

He stood there for a moment and looked at me. "Stop crying."

"No." I pushed him, but he didn't go anywhere. "Move!"

"Naw, we've done enough running. I'm not going anywhere. And neither are you."

"I need to find Shae."

"You need to chill."

"You don't understand. I'm leaving." I attempted to push past him. But instead of him letting me get by, he took the goose-down vest he wore over his Enyce hoodie, zipped it up, and enclosed me in it. Now we were chest to chest and I couldn't possibly move. "What are you doing?"

"I'm not letting you go. I want you to calm down."

All I could do was cry into his chest and explain to him in between my tears what happened. He wiped my eyes. "Shae'll come around, just give her a minute."

"I hope so." I looked up at him.

"Me, too." He held his head down and as if on instinct our faces moved toward one another. I closed my eyes and as if Christmas, New Year's, and the Fourth of July had all come at once, we kissed passionately, and for a moment I was able to forget everything bad that had existed.

9

Sittin' up in my room
I must confess I'm a mess for you . . .

—BRANDY, "SITTIN' UP IN MY ROOM"

I lay back on my bed with my bare feet pressed against the wall and my head turned to the side. The volume on my radio was low but the words to Aaliyah's "One In A Million" seduced my ears as if I were seeing her in concert, as my hot pink lava lamp illuminated my dark bedroom. Toi had been complaining about her bed making her back hurt, so she was in the living room asleep on the pull-out couch.

I kept looking at my red plastic phone shaped like a pair of lips, wondering why it hadn't rang. Josiah promised he would call after he came home from his game in south Jersey. I wish I had Shae to talk me through this, but being that she'd ex'd me out of her life, I was all alone. For a moment I wondered if she missed me as much as I missed her. I couldn't stand feeling like this and I knew that hearing Josiah's voice and making up with Shae was the only cure.

Just as the D.J. played Destiny Child's "T-Shirt," my phone rang . . . Wait a minute, the phone rang? Was my phone ringing? I quickly looked at the clock and it read two AM. For a moment I wondered if it was Shae calling. Then I looked down at the caller ID for confirmation. But it wasn't Shae, it was my longtime love—my boo to the ninth power—okay that was a lil' corny, right? Okay, I'll admit I'm being extra but I can't breathe and my heart is having a stroke. Should I be sexy or sleepy? Okay—okay—okay—okay—whatever I decide, I need to hurry up before he hangs up.

"Hello?" I said sleepily. I figured that was better than sounding the way I really felt.

"Seven," he said, "you 'sleep?"

"Yeah . . ." I made a sound like I was stretching. "I was."

"My fault. I can see you in school tomorrow," he said, about to hang up.

"No, you good. Wassup?" I wanted to scream, *Can't you tell I would've waited all night for you?!*

"You, that's wassup. Didn't I tell you I was gon' call?"

You sure did, I thought to myself, *and I was wondering what took you so long.*

"I know," he continued, "you were wondering what took me so long."

"No, actually I forgot." I hoped he couldn't tell I was lying through my teeth.

"You forgot?" He laughed a little. "How you gon' forget your man?"

I couldn't stop smiling and it seemed like the drops in my lava lamp were giving me a high-five. I wanted to scream but I knew I couldn't blow my cool. I was tempted to spit out, *Just tell me you love me boy,* but instead I took a deep breath and said, "Oh, so you my man now? Thanks for asking."

"You know how I do."

I knew I was about to sound stupid, but I had to ask, "How long have you been checking for me?"

"You not about to sweat yourself, are you?" He laughed.

"Would you tell me?"

"Ai'ight, ma, for a minute. I can't remember how long. I didn't keep track of the time. All I know is that I saw you on your porch this summer, smiling, and ever since then, I couldn't stop thinking about you."

"And what else?" I pressed. Heck, how often does a girl get the one man of her dreams to admit all of this?

"Ai'ight now, I'm not about to sit up here and gas you all night like some lil' punk and then when you get mad, I'm all on blast about how I was crying in your ear."

"Is that what you did with Deeyah? Cried in her ear?"

"You ain't ready for what I did with Deeyah."

Now that caught me off-guard. "Okay..." I stalled. "So what's your favorite color?"

Josiah fell out laughing. "There you go again. You like to avoid things, don't you? Why you always running?"

"I don't run. I get out of breath too easily, plus it sweats my hair out."

"Be serious." I could hear him trying not to laugh.

I took a deep breath. "Ai'ight, I run, sometimes, when I don't know what else to do. Or say—"

"That's not gon' solve your problems."

"No, but it makes it so I don't have to play my issues so close."

"Why don't you talk about what's on your mind?"

"Because right now there's a million things on my mind and it would take up too much time."

"I got all the time in the world for you," he said.

I didn't have a response, so I was quiet.

"Runnin' again, huh? Is that why you don't have a boyfriend," he said. "You ran 'em all away?"

"Ah un rudeness! No, you didn't. Me not having a boyfriend is a choice."

"And how long ago did you make that choice?"

"Last year."

"Last year?" He sounded as if he couldn't believe it. "Who you date last year? I ain't see nobody around you last year. But, you know"—he paused—"there was a rumor about you and Dollah. That's why I ain't kick it to you then."

I almost peed on myself. Dollah was the holdup to me fulfilling my destiny? "What are you talking about a rumor? You wait till I see Dollah and see don't I check his chin and slide him all at one time!"

"Dang, ma, I was just joking about the Dollah thing. Why you so sensitive? You liked him or something?"

"Why you say that?" I know I should've told the truth but I was too nervous to.

"I'm just asking."

"Well un-ask."

"Fall back, boo. I'm just sayin', if anything, now's the time to tell me, 'cause once you become wifey I'm not gon' wanna hear it."

"I thought you said you were my man already and besides, what difference does it make? You think you the only one that can like me?"

"Come on, ma, don't play me like that. You too fine for me to be the only one liking you. Know what, your voice is too sweet for you to be getting mad, so let's chill about the Dollah thing and tell me what happened with the last boyfriend you had. Where was he from?"

Why didn't I just tell the truth? "He lived

around the corner from me." I wanted to hurry and get off this subject. "Can we talk about something else?"

"Why? I wanna know why y'all broke up."

"Because I found out he was using me."

"Using you?"

"Yeah, I overheard him saying to his friends that he liked me because I spent all my money on him." I left out the giving up the booty part.

"Word?" Josiah asked.

"Word. He figured I was fat and needed him to be my boyfriend or something, so he tried to make me pay for him, literally."

"That's messed up."

"Plus he used to always tell me, 'You look good for a big girl. I likes me some big girls.' Big girls this and big girls that. After a while I was like dang, do you even know me?"

"So what, you don't like reppin' for the big girls?"

"No," I said a little too quickly. "I like to rep for me, Seven, and not for no big-behind girl." Why did I feel like I was about to cry? I cannot be this corny. "And if that's what you think or what you like me for, because you think I'm some stupid lil' fat chick looking to buy a boy's attention, you got me messed all the way up!"

"Wo, calm all that down, ma, 'cause I ain't ole boy and that's who you need to reserve all that extra base in your throat for. Now peep this, I'm diggin' you. Period. Yeah, you a lil' thick, but so what? You workin' it. You fly at all times. Me, I like your smile, the way you laugh with your eyes when you find something is funny. The way one of your dimples sits a little higher than the other. The way you fold your bottom lip into your mouth when you get nervous. I like you, the entire package of you. So don't ever come at me like that again. I just left a chick I could use, so I'm not looking for that. I'm checking for Seven, trying to make her my best friend and then my wife."

I must be a dummy, because tears were streaming from my eyes. I couldn't think of what to say next so I started to get this all over with and ask him to marry me.

"Ai'ight, Flo Jo"—he laughed—"'cause I know you looking for someplace to run—"

"Ai'ight, bye." Now I know I said that too fast, especially since I knew I wasn't gon' hang up that easily.

"Dang, well how long you been wantin' to hang up?"

"Well, I ain't mean to say it like that, but I figured since it was getting late"—I looked at the clock and over an hour had gone by—"you wanted to hang up since you had such a long day."

"Nah, you good, ma."

"Okay, so how was your game?"

Josiah and I talked for what felt like forever because I don't remember hanging up. And although I don't remember falling to sleep, I know that I just woke up and my alarm clock was going off, which meant it was six o'clock in the morning, so why was the phone still to my ear? That's when I realized that there was no dial tone and I could still hear breathing. "Josiah?" I said, wondering if he were still on the phone. "Josiah?"

"Yo . . . yeah . . ." he said groggily. "Wassup?"

"We fell asleep on the phone."

"I feel so violated," he joked.

"Ha—ha—ha. Funny."

"Yo, ma, I gotta go."

"Yeah, we gotta get ready for school."

"Ai'ight, now give me a kiss good-bye."

I pressed my lips to the phone and gave him a kiss.

"Dang, Seven, you need to go brush your teeth." He cracked up laughing.

"Oule, I'ma catch you dead in the face!"

"For real, ma, I was just playing. Here." He gave me a kiss through the phone. "Now I'll see you at school and don't tell nobody I was blowin' kisses through no phone either."

"Ai'ight, boy." My heart was doing a dance as I hung up. Not even my daddy could get on my nerves today. As I opened my bedroom door I could hear my parents in the kitchen laughing. A sound I hadn't heard in a long while. I eased out the bed, took a quick shower, and threw on a pair of khaki gauchos and a cap sleeve baby blue tee that read, "I Am A Dream." I slid on a pair of matching boots and headed into the kitchen to grab something to eat.

My sister was eating a bowl of cereal and both

of us were looking at my mother like she was crazy to be sitting up here grinning in my daddy's face, knowing that by the end of today he was flying back to Cali to be with another woman.

Shae was at the bus stop but she refused to speak to me. I sat in the front of the bus and she sat all the way in the back. All I could say to myself was how I wasn't going to cry. When we reached our destination she didn't even look my way. She hopped off the back of the bus and went inside the school.

After a few hours passed and three classes went by, it was time for lunch. I sat down at the table by myself with my tray of French fries, cheeseburger, and a coke sitting in front of me. This was the first time I'd eaten lunch alone since I was in the second grade, when one of the kid's lied and said I had three eyes.

"What, you got the cooties?" Josiah playfully frowned as he sat next to me.

"I might."

"Dang, guess I'm Mr. Cootie then, huh? Picture it, your friends gon' be calling our house, talkin' about 'Hey, Cootie.' "

I couldn't help but laugh. "You so corny, what's next? You wearing pink?"

"Ai'ight now, bring it back, Seven. You way out there."

"Uhmm hmm, I think you'd look cute in pink."

"Whatever . . . so why you ain't come sit with me?"

"'Cause I ain't wanna bother you and your friends."

"Man, forget my friends. I can chill with them any day." Josiah stroked my hair to the back and kissed me on the cheek. I looked at Shae, who'd just rolled her eyes at me. "She'll come around," he said. "Trust me. She misses you, too."

I sighed. "I guess you're right."

"Trust me, I know things."

I smiled and twisted my lips. "And what else you know?"

"I know you better eat that cheeseburger, before it's mine."

"You can have it."

He picked it up and took a bite. "Uhmm, this is good, ma. Taste it." He pressed it against my lips and the ketchup smeared my lip gloss.

My face lit up. "Would you stop it!" I slapped his hand.

"Bite it."

I bit a piece and started chewing. "That's good, ain't it, boo," he said. "That's wassup!"

I fell out laughing and looked at Shae, who I knew couldn't stand that she was smiling and laughing at me. She pointed to my chin and when I felt it, I had ketchup on it. "Let me get that for you," Josiah said, kissing it off.

"Boy," I said, "you better stop. You gon' mess around and get me suspended."

"Nah," he said with a serious face. "I'ma mess around and make you mine."

10

_____

"**Y**ou know you gon' help out with this project, right?" I nervously smiled as Josiah opened the front door of his house for me. He lived on Avon Avenue in one of the new split-levels that was recently built. I couldn't believe I was finally stepping into his spot and we hadn't officially put a title on our situation yet. I couldn't wait to see how he was going to introduce me to his mother.

For the last two and a half weeks, Josiah and I had grown really close. We talked on the phone everyday, ate lunch together, he gave me rides to work and home, and sometimes he would come by and we would sit in his car together and chill. For a minute it seemed like he was all I had. Shae still wasn't speaking to me; as a matter-fact, she changed her work days. I didn't have much to say to Toi, especially since I heard she was sneaking down to the county jail to see homeboy, who by the way tried to convince her to carry all the charges since she was still a minor. And other than coming home to see about Man-Man, my mother was purposely doing double shifts at work to avoid the stress of coming home. Needless to say I was holding my breath hoping I did a fierce job hooking my gear up, especially since I didn't have my usual fashion advice. Since it was chilly outside I wore a tangerine colored V-neck sweater, a brown leather braided belt wrapped around my waist, a fitted light blue denim miniskirt, wedge heel knee boots, and a hooded brown leather jacket with a big hobo bag. My orange plastic bracelets clapped together as I wiped invisible sweat from my brow and told myself to calm down.

Josiah looked me up and down as I stepped in his entrance way. "Dang, ma, who's your man? You look good."

"I don't have a man."

"Yeah, ai'ight," he said as I walked into his living room and admired his house. The style was Afrocentric and everything seemed to have its place. His mother was in the kitchen with her boyfriend laughing when I followed behind Josiah and he introduced me. "Ma, this is my friend, Seven." Hmph, his friend . . . Seven . . . no other title added on to my name, just Seven. Plain and simply, Seven. Ooookay . . . moving right along.

"Hey lil' mama, I know you. You sat next to me at the game, when Miss Mama wanted to show her behind." She rolled her eyes at Josiah. "Anyway, it's good to see you again, baby. This is my friend, Mr. Spenser." There's that word again, *friend*. Maybe that was a code word between Josiah and his mother; an understanding that the two of them had, one that maybe I didn't quite get just yet . . . especially since it was obvious that Mr. Spenser was more than just a friend. If nothing else, their body language spoke volumes: he was massaging her shoulders and her head was tossed back in the crux of his arm, as if his hands felt like silk . . . Maybe it was just me who didn't care for being called simply a friend.

"Ai'ight, ma, we going downstairs," Josiah said as he led me to the basement that was also his room. His room? Wait a minute, he was allowed to have company in his room? My mother woulda died, Cousin Shake would've passed out beside her, and my daddy, who had gone back to California and I was still avoiding every time he called, would've shown up for a special "my children are outta control" visit.

"Close the door," Josiah said as he dimmed the lights and cut the radio on, which ironically was playing Ciara's "And I." "You know this is our jam, right?" I smiled as I flicked the lights back on and closed the door.

"Oh, yeah?" This was the first time I'd ever seen him blush. "We got a jam?"

"Maybe."

"Maybe you should come here." He grabbed

me by one of the belt loops in my skirt as he sat on the edge of his bed.

"Maybe," I said as he pulled me toward him, "we should prepare your science project."

"Ai'ight"—he smiled—"that *is* why I called you over here."

"Yes"—my heart thundered—"you did."

"Actually it's not a project, it's a report," he said. "And it's a big part of my grade. So I have to do well, otherwise it'll put my basketball scholarship in jeopardy." He pulled his science books out of his backpack and sprawled them across the bed. He laid on his stomach and opened his notebook. "See, I have to do a report on the anatomy of the neurological system and what parts affect what parts, how, and why."

"Okay." I unzipped the sides of my boots, took them off, and lay down beside him. He was on his stomach and I was on my back, but we were face to face. "Let me see this book, since you looking to be upgraded." I laughed.

"You gon' upgrade me?" He kissed me. "What's higher than number one?"

I couldn't answer because we started kissing and the next thing I know he'd climbed on top of me, which I quickly decided wasn't the best decision . . . and not because I didn't want him there . . . but because for the first time it made me think of things I never really considered before. And the feeling of his hands rubbing the sides of my thighs

I knew would only take me places I would regret, so I broke our kiss and told him to get up.

"What, you scared?"

"No," I said as he resumed his original position. "I'm just not ready for that."

"Ai'ight." He paused. "Let's do this report then."

"Cool. Now before we start, I wanna know what does a science grade have to do with a basketball scholarship?"

"Because"—he gave me a quick peck—"like the scouts that are seeking me out said, I need to pull up my G.P.A. a little more in order to get my scholarship and I'm lacking in science. Plus I wanna get into Syracuse bad."

"You looking at any other colleges?"

"Yeah, NC, A&T, Seton Hall, Rutgers. But I want Syracuse the most."

"So then you have to work for it, and since you tryna become Shaq, then let's make an outline of what's needed for your report so you can get an A."

"I surpassed Shaq, ma. I'm Josiah Whitaker, number twenty-three. Understand that."

"You can stop feeling yourself."

He stared at me. "Can we get back on the subject?"

"Yeah, and let me get out your face." I handed him back his notebook. "Your mind is everywhere but where it needs to be."

I climbed on his back, laid down, and placed

my head over his right shoulder. We were now cheek to cheek. "Let me know if I'm breaking your back."

"How you gon' break my back and I weigh more than you do? What you trippin' off of? You cool, ma."

Was he trying to say I wasn't fat? I'm not sure. But if I'm not fat then what am I?

Since I didn't exactly know what type of response I should come back with, I started reading his notes out loud with him.

By the time I helped Josiah finish his outline, I realized that I had actually done it.

"Don't make a habit out of me doing your work for you." I kissed him on the side of his forehead.

"Whatever." He smiled.

I climbed off his back. "I think I should be getting ready to go."

He looked at the clock, which read six-thirty. "It's not that late, you can stay a little while longer."

"Josiah . . ." I whined.

"Ai'ight, cool. If you wanna leave, it's not a problem."

"I'll stay . . . but just a little while longer." I sighed while looking around his room—which was the typical boy's room—posters on the wall, clothes piled in the corner, a full-sized bed, a futon, stereo, flat-screen TV, a few basketballs, and mountains of sneakers and Timbs. "So"—I picked up one of his basketballs—"how long you been ballin'?"

He held his palms up for me to toss him the ball, which I did. "For about as long as you been alive." He made a shot and the ball went through the basketball net hanging on the back of his door. "Swoosh!! And the crowd goes wild . . . !"

"Because it's the opposing team's basket!"

"Funny!" He slid off the bed.

I picked up the ball and started dribbling before making a shot. "You know you really can't play that well," I teased him. "Your game is like this." I waved my right hand from side to side.

"Ohhhh . . ." I could tell I caught him off-guard. "Is that so? Well, you talkin' a lotta smack for someone who couldn't even dream up how to ball." He got behind me and squatted as if he were guarding me. I dribbled and moved around his floor, then I did a spin and threw the ball over his shoulder right into the basket.

"And now the crowd really goes wild!" I said as I profiled. Once I saw he was trying to take the ball from me, I grabbed it off the floor and started dribbling again. "Booyah! And what?!" I made a quick shot.

"You so corny." He laughed while recovering the ball and tossed it back to me.

And just as I posed to make a basket, he stole the ball from me. "Oh, no, you didn't?!"

"I thought you had game?" He winked his eye.

"Ai'ight," I said as I watched him prepare to take a shot with one hand. Before he released the ball I snatched it back.

He stood up straight. "Oh, you got that off," he said, staring at me. And by the look he was giving, I could tell he was undressing me with his eyes and I didn't exactly want him to stop.

"What you lookin' at?" I smiled.

"You."

"So what you lookin' at me for?"

"Come 'mere, let me show you." He walked over and grabbed me around the waist. We started kissing passionately and I couldn't resist. I felt his hands traveling up my sweater and I knew I should've pushed them down sooner, but it took me a few seconds to go through with it. And I was able to do it without breaking our lip lock . . . Then I felt him unzip my skirt and I stopped.

"I'm not ready for that." His nose was buried in my neck.

"It's cool, ma." He gave me one last peck. "But you way too hot to keep the goodies on lock."

Now I knew it was time to go. "Can you take me home?"

"Why?"

"It's just getting late, that's all."

"It's late or you scared of what you may do?"

"I'm not answering that."

"Yo, I really don't want you to go." He held my

hand. "Let's just chill, watch a movie or something, but don't leave . . . just yet."

I hated that he was so cute. "You gon' keep your hands to yourself." He placed one hand behind his back and I could see him cross his fingers. "Cross my heart and hope to die."

"You know I see you, right?"

He laughed, removing his hand from behind his back. "For real, let's chill."

"Ai'ight." I grabbed a couple of his DVDs from his nightstand, plopped down in the middle of his bed, and crossed my legs Indian style. "So, what we gon' watch?" And as I looked through his collection of movies, I noticed I'd picked up a New York Yankees scully. I tried it on. "How do I look?" I shot Josiah a Kodak smile.

Josiah turned around and the smile he wore quickly faded. "Take that off!" he barked at me.

I was caught completely off-guard. "I'm sorry." I placed it back on the table.

Josiah stood still and stared at me for a moment. "My fault. I shouldn't have snapped at you like that."

"I didn't mean anything by that."

"I know"—he paused—"it's just that . . . that was my brother's hat. He had it on when he died."

I couldn't believe Josiah had tears in his eyes. I got off the bed and walked over to give him a hug. "I know you miss him."

"Yeah, it's been almost two years now."

"How's it been around the house since he died?"

142

"Quiet," he said. "It's been real quiet."

"I understand if you don't wanna watch the movie anymore."

"Come on, ma, it's cool. I'm enjoying you. I'm not ready to end the night."

"Okay." I sat back in the center of his bed Indian style. "So let's see . . . *Love Jones.*"

"I don't think so. No chick movies."

"It's your movie." I frowned.

"No, it's your mother-in-law's movie. She left it here when she was burning a copy for her friend. So you see that ain't me. No *Love Jones.*"

"And why not?"

"It's a chick movie."

"I wanna see it." I gave him the magical face.

He stared at me for a moment. "Ai'ight, Seven." He took the movie from my hand. "We can watch it this one time. But don't tell nobody. Got me up in here, watching *Love Jones,*" he mumbled as he slid the DVD in.

He sat behind me on his bed, locked his fingers around my waist, and for the next hour and a half we watched the movie.

After a while it was time for me to go. "Before we go"—Josiah pointed to his dresser—"look in my topdrawer and take out a white tee."

I did what he asked and then I held his shirt in my hand. "What you want me to do with this?"

Ni-Ni Simone

"I want you to keep it. Then I'll feel like I'm always with you."

"Awwl," I whined. "Josiah . . ." My heart was fluttering in my chest.

"I know"—he blushed—"give it to me." He puckered his lips and patted his cheek. "Right there."

"Now you want me to kiss you on the cheek?" I had to laugh. "The cheek? I said let's slow down and I ain't say let's drop dead." I walked up to him and gave him a peck on the lips. "I can't stand that I like you."

He threw his arm around the back of my neck and placed me in a pretend headlock. "What you mean like? You love me, girl."

I walked in the house and went in my room. My sister was laying in her bed, watching TV. "What you watching?" I asked.

"*Run's House.* Where you been?"

"Josiah's." I started undressing.

"Mommy know that?"

"Mommy hasn't been here to know much of anything. Ever since I saw her kiss Daddy when he left she's been doing crazy overtime."

"And I saw him sneaking out of her room," Toi added. "But that's their business. We have to deal with our own broken hearts."

"True." I slipped on Josiah's tee and I loved that I could smell him.

"So what's up with Josiah?"

I blushed. "Nothing."

"Yes, it is." She smiled. "I see you rockin' his white tee."

"Anyway"—I blushed—"before we talk about Josiah, I wanna know what you did all day." I looked at her stomach and noticed she was getting a little pouch. For the first time, I realized I was going to be an auntie and wondered if I would have a niece or a nephew.

"My lawyer's office, the doctor's"—she paused—"and to see Qua."

I rolled my eyes in my head. "What did the doctor say?"

"He said I was four months."

"Wow, four months and you're just finding out?"

"That's what the doctor said."

"So, what did your lawyer say?"

"He said . . . I'll probably get community service since I'm a minor and this is my first offense."

"Did you tell your boyfriend?"

"I did."

"And . . ." Not that I really wanted to hear what he said, but I could tell she wanted to tell me.

I couldn't believe it but tears filled her eyes. "He told me . . . he hated me."

"What?! Why?"

"Because I wouldn't take the charges. He said I was nothing but a stupid little girl that he shoulda never been caught up with, that he shoulda stayed with his oldest son's mother."

"So what you gon' do? You gon' stay with him?"

"No." She sniffed. "I don't think I could even if I wanted to . . ."

I was speechless and all I could do was sit on the edge of my sister's bed as she held her pillow tight to her face and cried her heart out.

11

Where my girls at . . .

—702, "WHERE MY GIRLS AT"

"Okay, Shae, how about this," I said as I stood in her bedroom doorway. "You just gon' have to call the cops to move me, 'cause I ain't leaving." It was seven o'clock in the morning and I got up extra early to come over here and make up with my best friend. I absolutely couldn't take not speaking to her anymore, and more than anything I needed her to forgive me.

She ignored me and instead of responding she searched through her closet for something to wear. She pulled out a cream hoodie with tiny hot pink skulls all over it, a pair of jeans, and a pair of denim Converse. "You know that's my hoodie," I said.

"Well, I'm wearing it," she snapped as she slipped it on. "And what?"

"Ooops, and nothing. Because actually this yellow hoodie I have on is yours, but the jeans are mine."

"I know." She slipped on her clothes and pulled out her jewelry box.

"I was wondering where my silver bracelets were."

"On my arm." She slid them on.

"Excuse me." I laughed. I looked her up and down and said, "You look cute."

"I know this." She looked at me. "You okay, but you need to take off those gold earrings and put these on." She tossed me a pair of yellow hoops. I slid them on and looked at her. "Now," she said with an attitude, "you look kinda fly."

"Thank you."

"Well, I'm headed to school, I gotta catch the bus." She rolled her eyes at me. "You comin'?"

"Only if you'll accept my apology and we become best friends again." We walked out her room and out the front door.

"I accepted it last week, when I was watching you and Josiah act like Reverend Run and his wife."

"Ha—ha—ha," I said sarcastically.

"Besides, we never stopped being best friends. I just wasn't talking to you."

"Really?" We started walking to the bus stop.

"Yes, really."

"Well, what happened last week that caused you to forgive me?"

"Ki-Ki. She felt bad and ended up telling me

the truth." Shae waved her hand so the bus knew to stop and we hopped on.

"Oh, get outta here. But I'm still not speaking to her."

"Me either," Shae said, "but all I cared about was that I had my sister back."

I looked at Shae and hugged her. "Ai'ight, girl I can't breathe."

I couldn't stop smiling. "I love you Boo-Boo," I whined.

"Yeah," she said as we stepped off the bus. "Hurry and tell me what's up with Josiah so I can tell you about Melvin."

"What's up with Big Country?"

"My daddy loves him."

"For real?" I couldn't stop smiling.

"Yeah, so wassup with my brother-in-law? Is it official yet?"

"I'm not sure. He hasn't asked me to be his girl-friend, but he treats me like wifey and he intro-duced me to his mother."

"Oh, if you met Mom, dukes you in there. Maybe he's kinda shy to ask. Actions speak louder than words anyway."

"True . . . so . . . let me ask you something."

"What?"

I twisted my lips. "You ever think about sex?"

"With who? Bow Wow? I give him some every night."

"Be for real, Shae." I laughed.

"Oh, you mean the real deal?"

"Yes."

"Well, yeah, I have and I made up my mind I'm not doing that, not yet anyway. I'ma tryna stay focused. I see enough chicks our age pregnant, so I'm good and if Melvin can't stay calm with a lil' kiss and maybe an extra feel then he gotta do what he gotta do and I'll just have to deal with it."

"That's a way to look at it."

"Don't tell me"—she squinted her eyes—"you gave it up to Josiah?! Dang, Seven, you just started going with him. I can't believe you did that!"

"Can you calm down? The only thing I gave Josiah was a kiss, nothing else."

"You sure?" Shea said as we got off the bus.

"What you mean am I sure? Why would I lie to you of all people?"

"Oh, true."

"I just been thinking about it."

"Is he pressuring you?"

"Sorta, but he didn't ask right out."

"Just tell him," she said as we walked in the side entrance of the school, "that you're not ready yet and he needs to wait."

"Yeah." I nodded my head as we prepared to go our separate ways. "Maybe . . . maybe that's exactly what I'll do."

12

Josiah and I and Shae and Melvin had been a couple for four months and we were celebrating our four month anniversary at Arizona's together. Arizona's was nothing fancy and it looked to be the type of place that was virtually unchanged since before I was born. Actually my mother said this was where she met my father for the first time and from the sounds of it, nothing in here has changed except the people who hung out here and the music.

There were about five square tables covered with plastic floral tablecloths, red leather kitchen chairs with silver duct tape on the back to hold some of the torn leather together, a worn wooden bar with two pitchers of Uptown on it, and a cuss box, where you were charged a quarter for any curse word you said. And if you mixed the word God in with a curse there was no quarter to be paid, you just had to leave. And there were five pool tables, all lined up in a row.

"Cornbread," Melvin said to Shae as he tried to show her how to position her pool stick, "this a grown man's game and I need you to learn how to play quick."

"You know how to hold your stick?" Josiah looked at me with concern. "'Cause all that Big Country doing, I wit' that. He may as well play the game for her."

"Ah un rudeness," I said, sipping my soda. "No, you didn't?! Not in front of company."

"Look"—I could hear Melvin, as he tried his best to whisper to Shae—"how we 'spose to beat them if you shakin' like a leaf. You know the stakes, loser pays for the movies later and let me tell ya somethin', Moms been comin' up short on the allowance. Don't play with me."

"Big Country," Shae whined, "I'm tryin'."

All I could do was smile. This was gon' be a cinch. "I tell you what," I said, "why don't we switch partners—"

"Awwl nawl, Shawtie," Melvin said. "This ain't *Wife Swap*. I'm not one of them dudes."

Oh I hate him! I rolled my eyes. "That's not what I mean."

"Oh," Melvin said, "then say what you mean, Shawtie."

"I mean let's switch teams. Me and Shae verses you and Josiah."

Smiles ran across Josiah and Melvin's faces. They just knew they had this in the bag. I looked at Shae and winked my eye. Little did Josiah and Melvin know but we had somethin' for 'em. "I tell you what," I said to Melvin and Josiah as Melvin racked the balls, "the loser has to pay the winner twenty dollars and pay for the movies."

"It's cool," Josiah said. "We'll take the challenge."

He nudged Melvin and they looked at Shae who was holding the pool stick backwards, pretending to take a shot. "Ladies first," Josiah said as laughter eased out the side of his mouth.

"Want me to hold the stick for you, Cornbread," Melvin snickered.

"You would do that for me, Pooh." Shae smiled at him. "Why don't you and Josiah go first so I can watch y'all."

"Yeah," I whined while pretending to agree. "Y'all go first."

"Ai'ight." Melvin broke the balls and knocked a solid one in the pocket.

"Oh," Shae said, "is that where that goes?"

Josiah passed me so he could take a shot. "Don't worry," he said, "I'll take my twenty dollars in installments."

Josiah's ball didn't go in the pocket so now it was our turn. "Shae, you can go first."

Shae positioned herself and then she looked at

the table. "Hmph," she said, "here goes." She took a shot and knocked two of our balls in at one time. Then it was my turn and I knocked two more balls in.

"Whew," I said, watching Melvin and Josiah's mouths fly open. "Now what am I gon' do with my twenty dollars?"

As I walked past Josiah to the other side of the table I lifted up his bottom lip. "Close your mouth."

Shae winked at me, took a shot, and knocked her ball in the socket. "I'ma hustlah, I'ma—I'ma hustlah, baby . . . better ask about me."

The game was over in ten minutes. Shae and I stood side by side and held our palms out. "Pass off our money."

13

Everybody knows that almost doesn't count . . .

—BRANDY, "ALMOST DOESN'T COUNT"

The teachers had an in-service day, which meant one thing: Newark Tech got out at noon and we were home chillin'. I purposely didn't tell my mother that I had a half day because I didn't want her sweatin' me about what to do around the house since I was home early, what to take out the refrigerator, and so forth. The best thing that could've happened to me was that no one was here but me and Shae. My mother was working double shift, Man-Man was in school, and Cousin Shake was chillin' with his fifty-year-old tender.

In between eating Chinese crabsticks and French fries, Shae and I danced over and over again to Brandy's remix of "I Wanna Be Down." This jam mighta been old but it was poppin' and the CD player in my living room was working Lyte and Latifah's part all the way out. I felt like we were at a throwback party. We were doing every move you could think of from the Chicken Noodle Soup to the Wu-tang to the revitalized Electric Slide. Both of us felt like we were partying on cloud nine. After all, we were on a high. We both had boos and not just any ole boos, but boos that chilled together and were friends. The only way to describe this feeling was to call it fiyah!

For the last few weeks I was doing my best to ignore Josiah's not so subtle hints about wantin' some. Heck, in my mind I had a wedding to plan, even if it couldn't happen for at least another ten years.

When Brandy sang "I could be wrong but I feel like something could be going on," Shae lost her mind and started doing dances that I had never seen before. I stopped dancing, stood back, and looked at her like she was crazy. "Has Big Country ran away with your mind?"

She laughed. "Girl, you just don't know. There ain't no other for me!" She started doing the snake and then she broke it down and started break dancing on the floor.

I couldn't stop laughing at Shae's dancing and just as she broke out into a spin, the phone rang. "Hello?"

"Wassup, ma?"

It was Josiah and immediately all the butterflies in my stomach started groovin'. "You, that's wassup."

"Your mother home?"

"No." Now I know I'm not supposed to have no company when nobody's home, but dang that would sound so corny.

"Your mom's gon' bug if me and my boy Big Country come chill over there? I know Shae is there."

I turned around and looked at Shae who was break dancing on the floor. "Yeah, she here. And please"—I lied—"my moms is cool."

"Straight, then we gon' come through."

"Ai'ight, do that."

"Give me a kiss."

I gave him a kiss through the phone. "That's what I'm talking about," he said as he hung up.

I turned the music down. "Get off the floor. We need to fix our hair and retouch our makeup. We got some future baby daddies comin' over."

Before we could bum-rush the bathroom, the doorbell rang. Toi must've lost her keys again. My mother is gon' get sick of changing these locks. I opened the door and oh . . . my . . . God, it wasn't Toi, it was Dollah. I looked at him like he was crazy. What the heck was he doing at my door?!

"Somethin' we need to talk about?" I asked Dollah as he stood in my doorway. I was blocking his path like I lived in Ft. Knox or something because there was no way he was coming up in here.

"Yo, what's good?" he asked, smiling at me.

"It ain't you." I frowned. "Now what is it?"

"Fall back, Seven, dag. I came by for two reasons—"

"Well, one of them need to be to apologize," Shae said. "Ain't nobody forgot about you, Clyde."

"It's Dollah," he snapped. "Anyway, Seven, let's just try and get over what happened between us. My fault for not treating you the way I should've."

"Whatever."

"Ai'ight, Seven, whatever."

"I just came by to get my ring," he said.

"Just wait a minute." I went in my room, grabbed his ring from my jewelry box, came back out, and handed it to him.

"Thank you, ma." He stepped in a little too close to me.

"Let me see your hand." Before I could say no, he lifted my right hand and slid his ring on my married finger. "That's lookin' real fly, ma. Now how you gon' take that off?"

"I don't see where it would be that hard," Josiah said as he stepped into my living room. I could've peed on myself. My heart was thundering like it was about to be World War III up in my mother's living room and Lawd knows I could'nt have no bombs go off, especially since I'm not supposed to have nobody over here.

"Here," I said to Dollah, practically pulling my finger off and shoving the ring into his hand. "Now, bye."

"Ai'ight, ma." He gave Josiah a smirk. "It's always a pleasure."

The veins on the side of Josiah's neck jumped

as he clenched his jaw tightly. He watched Dollah walk out the door and then he turned to me. "Let me hollah at you for a minute, Shortie."

"Shortie?" I joked. "You been hanging around Melvin too long." I guess it wasn't funny because no one laughed but me . . . and even that wasn't genuine.

I followed Josiah to my room where I closed the door and then looked out my window. "Was it cold outside?"

"Peep this, and peep it real quick. You got two seconds to tell me the deal with ole dude or I'ma step off."

"What?" Was he about to break up with me over Dollah? "What do you mean you gon' step off?" I gave him the magical look. "You breaking up with me?"

"The look ain't gon' work."

"So what you sayin'?"

"I'ma sayin', I'ma bounce—me and you—about to be through. Now I'ma ask you again, wassup with you and this dude?"

"Remember"—I sighed—"I told you about my boyfriend last year . . ."

"Yeah."

"It was"—I stalled a little—"Dollah."

"Dollah? Dollah was your boyfriend? The one that lied on you?"

"Yeah."

"So you still feeling this dude?"

"No! Heck, no! He was over here to get his ring. I didn't invite him over here, he just showed up."

"I can't believe this, you and Dollah? You know I can't stand that dude and this is what you do? You play me for him? So what, you wanna bounce and be with him, 'cause I'm not about to battle Dollah for no chick!"

My feelings were hurt but I knew I had to come back. "Battle for me?" I couldn't believe he said that. "You ain't gotta battle for me. As a matter-fact, we ain't even gotta be together." I swear I hope he didn't call my bluff. " 'Cause right about now you actin' real ridiculous. I swear to you I'm not even checkin' for that dude."

"Then why you lie to me, when I asked you were you checking for him?"

"Because I didn't wanna take the chance of you not wanting to be with me, but I was going to tell you. I almost did."

"Yeah, and my brother almost didn't get in that car."

"What?"

"Seven, ma, look, I'm out."

"I'm not with him! I'm with you."

He stared at me for a moment. "You wifey?"

"Yeah," I said, doing my best to suppress a smile. "You know that."

"Well, let me tell you the first rule to staying wifey—don't lie to me. Now, I'll hollah," Josiah said as he walked out of my room.

"Josiah," I called behind him but he ignored me.

"Yo, Big Country," Josiah said. "I'm 'bout to bounce. You comin'?"

"Yeah, I need to help my moms with something anyway." He gave Shae a peck on her forehead. "Stay pretty."

Shae couldn't stop cheesing long enough to notice the tears in my eyes.

Once Melvin and Josiah left, I broke down and cried. "What happened?" Shae said in a panic.

"He said"—I shivered and my chest heaved— " 'I'll hollah'."

"What does that mean?" Shae asked.

"I don't know," I cried. "I really don't know."

For the first time ever on a school morning I didn't need my alarm clock to wake up, because I'd been up all night crying. My eyes were puffy and I had a headache. And since I was depressed I wanted to dress the opposite of how I felt, so I threw on a fitted cream thermal, a brown corduroy miniskirt, multicolored tights decorated with flowers and stripes, and a pair of brown suede boots. My hair was hanging down, flat-ironed straight, with a cream silk scarf tied around the front like a headband.

I decided not to eat breakfast but instead take the early bus to school. I figured Shae would get the hint when she didn't see me. So I grabbed my off-white goose down coat and pulled the drawstrings tight to my waist, picked up my backpack and was on my way.

"Dang, retardo," Man-Man said on my way out the door. "What, the special ed kids testing early today?"

I felt so sad I didn't even respond.

"Bubble Butt, you're not gon' say nothin'? Oh man, what's wrong?" He ran up and hugged me from behind. "Come sit down and talk to me."

I looked at him, gritted my teeth, and said, "Move! Get yo' stinkin' self away from me and go put on some deodorant."

"Maaaaa!" he cried, running toward my mother who'd just come in the house from work. "Did you tell them I was stinking the other day?"

"What are you talking about, Man-Man?" my mother snapped. "Why would I tell somebody that?"

"Then why she say to put on some deodorant? I take the best wash-up I can in the morning," he cried.

I turned to him and said, "And that's why you stink!"

As soon as I arrived at the bus stop, the bus had just pulled up and was loading with passengers. After I paid my fare, I would've usually gone straight to the back, but today I took the first seat I found.

I really couldn't believe this was happening to me. My relationship with Josiah had gone by so fast and the hurt that I thought I could cry away still stung in my chest like lightning. The invisible fist in my throat pressed against my tonsils like a migraine and for a moment I wondered if I would ever recuperate.

I pressed the buzzer so I could get off at my stop and as the doors opened, Josiah was sitting on the hood of his parked car. I rolled my eyes up to the sky.

"Come 'mere," he said as I attempted to pass by. There was no way I could let him know he'd hurt my feelings. He pulled slightly on my arm. "Where you going?"

I put up a little resistance but not much.

"What?" I wiggled my neck and sucked my teeth as he pulled me close. "I thought you were hollerin'."

"And I did." He held me around the waist. "How long did you think I was gon' stay away? A night was enough for you to get the point."

"So what, I was on punishment?"

"Yep, but I ended up punishing myself because I picked up the phone like a hundred times to call you. You missed me?"

"Uhmm hmmm." I sucked my teeth. I was doing my all not to laugh, but he looked so cute, dressed in his red North Face bubble jacket, red baseball cap, black jeans, and matching Tims.

"You know you wanna smile."

I could tell my dimples gave it away, so I turned my face.

"Don't lie to me no more. I hate lies. The last time my brother lied and said he was only going to the store, he never came back."

"I'ma always come back."

"You better." He reached in his pocket and took out a gold box with a white bow on top.

I reached for the box.

"Naw." He waved the box in front of me. "These for wifey."

"So I ain't wifey no more?"

"I don't know, you tell me." He handed me the box and when I took off the top, there were two heart-shaped bamboo earrings with "Wifey" written in big script letters in the center of each of them. I held the box to my chest with my arms crossed and before I could get a hold of myself, I was hugging the box as if it were a long lost cousin.

"Can I get some of that?" Josiah asked.

"Ohhhhh." I opened my arms and he moved into my embrace.

"You still wifey?" he asked as I held him tight.

"Yes," I said as we began kissing. "I ain't gon' never stop being wifey."

14

Girl it would be fly
If you were my
B.U.D.D.Y. . . .

—MUSIQ SOULCHILD, "B.U.D.D.Y."

Okay, so . . . my body was all prepared to give away my virginity but my mind was scared. Although Josiah hadn't come right out and asked for some, I could tell by the comments he'd been making when I would go over to his house or he would see me in the school's hallway and we would sneak a midmorning kiss, that he wanted us to smash. I could almost see myself doing it, but just when I wanted to take his hand and lead him home, I would always punk out.

"Can I ask you something, Toi?" I said as we lay in our beds in the dark. It was about twelve-thirty at night and for the first time in a long time my sister wasn't crying herself to sleep.

"What you wanna ask me?"

"How was it the first time?"

"How was what the first time?" She turned over

to look at me. The street lights that snuck in through our mini-blinds made stripes across her pregnant body and shadowed onto the floor.

"You know . . ."

"No, I don't."

I took a deep breath. "The first time you—you had sex—how was it?"

"You're not thinking about sleeping with Josiah, are you?"

"Well . . . yes. Yeah . . . I am."

"Why?" she asked as if she were surprised. "Why would you do that?"

"Because I care about him. And he wants to."

"And you want to?"

"Maybe."

"I hope you don't think having sex with him is going to make him stick around, do you?"

"No—yes—no—I don't know."

"Well, do you, 'cause I gave it up and I'm sitting here alone, so if I were you, I'd cancel that thought."

"I love Josiah."

"Whatever, you'll see."

"But I really do love him."

"Then get you some birth control."

"No, and no thank you."

"And you call me stupid. Alright, so . . . are you ready to be a mother, then?"

"Girl, please."

"Well, you must wanna be pregnant, because you talking about sex and no birth control."

"I know my cycle, thank you. And there's such a thing called the rhythm method, or he could pull out."

"Uhmmm." She twisted her lips. "You know what they call people that do that?"

"What?"

She pointed to her stomach. "Parents. Just skip the heartache and buy you some Trojans."

I couldn't get over the way Toi was talking to me. "Don't look at me crazy," she said. "This real talk. Let me ask you this—is he HIV-positive or does he have any other disease?"

"What kinda . . . question is that?!" I was convinced she'd lost her mind. "Never mind, Toi."

"What you mean, never mind? You asked me. Sex is not a game." She pointed to her stomach. "Obviously."

"You've had sex and you don't have HIV or any other STD."

"You don't know that. You can't tell that by looking at me, the same way you can't tell that by looking at him."

"So what, you a magazine ad now?"

"No, I'm your sister. Hell, Qua could've had an STD, but I was so caught up that I didn't even think about it. I just assumed because I loved him he was automatically disease-free."

"So when did you think differently?"

"When my OB/GYN tested for all these STDs and I was worried for days."

"But you don't have anything. Do you?"

"No, I don't. Thank God. But suppose I did? Then what? It would be too late, which is why I'm saying this to you now. Don't make a life-altering decision just because you feeling a dude."

"That's a bit dramatic, don't you think?"

"No, I think being pregnant at sixteen is dramatic. I think making the right decision is being smart. Look at me and learn." She rubbed her pregnant belly. "I'm what happens when you don't listen."

Before I could respond, there was a knock on our bedroom door. "Seven," my mother called. "Toi?"

"Yes," we both said.

"Ma," I asked, "you just getting off work?"

"Not really. I was standing at your door for a minute."

Oh, God, I figured she must've been in here to go off. "So what you think, Ma? What do you have to say because I know you listened to our conversation."

"Some of it. I caught the tail end mostly."

"So what you think?"

"I think your sister told you the right thing. And I think I better stop working so much before I miss how I've raised two beautiful young ladies. Now come give your mother a hug."

We got up and each gave her a hug so tight that we fell onto my bed. "We gon' get through this." My mother kissed Toi on the forehead. "And you," she said to me, "you listen to what your sister said."

"Maaaa . . ."

"Seven, I'ma hold off on judgment. But I'm warning you, don't try me."

15

Stop . . . Go . . .
So confusing that I don't know why I wanna ask why . . .

—FAITH EVANS, "STOP N GO"

"Now you know," Josiah said to me, "that you ain't got all that delicious junk in yo' trunk by ordering no garden salad . . ." He turned to the waitress. "Give her a steak." *Was that a compliment?*

We were at Applebee's on Rt. 22 eating dinner. It was Valentine's Day and we were celebrating. We'd just come back from the movies and neither one of us were ready to go home. "I know you didn't just try and call me fat?"

"Huh?" He arched one eyebrow higher than the other. "Who you talkin' to? Who called you fat, so I can handle that." He looked around the restaurant.

"I'm talking to you."

"Nah, ma, you couldn't be talking to me, because I don't date fat chicks. Now if you thick, we can kick it."

"Okay, Josiah, whatever."

"Real talk, keep it funky, why you buggin'?"

"Buggin' about what?"

"This imaginary weight thing. Where did that come from?"

I hunched my shoulders.

"For real, ma, chill out wit' that. 'Cause as I see it, weight is not an issue. From where I'm sittin' you bangin', which is why I hurried up and wifed you."

This was the first time in my life that words had meant so much to me. I tried to show appreciation with my eyes. "That was sooooo sweet."

"You know how I do it."

"Whatever," I said as I stood up from my seat. We were in a booth and I was directly across from him.

"Where you going?" he asked.

"Next to you." I slid next to him.

"For what? What you want?" he asked suspiciously.

"I wanna kiss."

"What you wanna kiss me for?" He pressed his lips against mine.

We kissed for a few seconds before the waitress came over. I could hear her clearing her throat as she sat our plates in front of us.

I picked up a French fry from my plate and stuck it in his mouth. My finger felt warm sliding off his tongue. "Why you feeding me, ma?" he asked.

" 'Cause you so cute."

"True." He smiled. "If I'ma be your man, I gotta be fly."

I stared at him for a few minutes. There's no way this was real.

"What?" he asked. "What you thinking about?"

"How I'ma be when you leave me."

I could tell he was taken aback. "Where I'm goin', ma?"

"I don't know, somewhere—anywhere—if my daddy could leave me and Mother, move to California, and have a whole 'nother family, then anything is possible."

"Well, I'm not your father. I'm your man and I ain't leaving you."

"Promise?"

"Cross my heart and hope to die."

"You so corny," I said as I continued to feed him, "real—real corny."

"And you love it."

"Every bit of it."

16

I only got four minutes . . .

—Avant

Shae and I were on our way to the movies when we ran into Dollah and a few of his boys on the corner of Bergen Street.

"What, you gon' act like you don't see me, Seven?" he asked as I tried to hurry by.

"No"—I threw over my shoulder—"I'm not gon' act like I don't see you, I'ma act like I don't hear you." And Shae and I proceeded to cross the street.

Before we could make it through the crosswalk, Dollah was on my heels. "What do you want?" I asked him as we stood on the corner.

"And make it quick," Shae snapped. "We don't need no problems." She pointed to Deeyah, Ki-Ki, and Yaanah who were walking up the street.

"Yo, I just wanted to know if you were going to the Seniors' dance."

"I'm not goin' with you. Why don't you ask Deeyah, ain't that who you kickin' it to?"

"Naw, she just a lil' somethin' to do. But you a good girl, Seven, and I'm tryna see you."

"Don't you have a boyfriend?" Deeyah walked up behind me. I almost forgot she was coming up the street.

"Don't you have your own business to mind?"

"I would mind it if I could keep you out of it. Seems like all the men I get you trying to pick up."

"Well, you should stop losing 'em."

"Go 'head, Deeyah," Shae warned, " 'cause you know I don't talk first."

"Whoool, I'm scared."

"Yo, listen," Dollah said, "hollah at me when you get a minute." And he walked away.

"Hey, Shae. Hey, Seven," Ki-Ki and Yaanah said.

"You hear that?" Shae asked.

"No." I blinked my eyes. "I didn't."

"I didn't think so." And we walked on to the movies.

"You better call Dollah when you get home and check that fool. You know everybody know Josiah, and somebody is bound to tell 'em."

"Yeah, that hatin'-behind Deeyah."

"Exactly, 'cause she want him back anyway. So you better tell ole boy to cool out."

"Yeah, you right." But before I could go on, my cell phone rang. It was Josiah. "Oh, my God"—I turned to Shae—"it's him. Dang, she couldn't wait to call him. What I'm 'spose to do? What I'm 'spose to say?"

"Nothing. Like Ciara said, 'Act like a boy.' Don't say a thing. If he doesn't mention it, then you don't either."

"And if he does?"

"Get amnesia. Act like you don't know what he talking about."

"Okay." I took a deep breath. "Hey, Boo-Boo," I answered.

"Can you come through?"

Oh, God, I think he knows. "When you want me"—I paused—"to come?"

"Now."

"Josiah . . ." I sighed.

"I mean it's cool if you can't come through," he said. "If you doing something more important than being with me."

"No . . . it's that me and Shae were . . ."

"I said it's cool, Seven."

"Give me an hour, I'll be there." And I hung up. I just knew Shae was gon' be ticked off.

"Shae"—I paused—"Josiah wants to see me now."

"You serious?" she asked. "You know Deeyah called him, right. Probably as soon as she turned the corner good she was in his ear."

"You not mad? What about the movies?"

"No, girl, I ain't mad. I wanted to see my boo anyway. I miss me some Big Country."

* * *

I got to Josiah's house in less than an hour after he called. When I rang the bell, his mother opened the door for me. She looked to be on her way out. "Hey, Sweetie."

"Hi, Ms. Whitaker."

"Josiah's in the dining room at the bar," she said. "I tried to tell him it's not the end of the world, but he's just like his father was, doesn't wanna hear a thing. Anyway, I'm going, sweetie."

"Ms. Whitaker, what's wrong with Josiah?"

"I thought you knew . . . well, let him tell you." She waved bye and closed the door behind her.

When I walked into the dining room, it was mostly dark, except for the light sneaking in from the slits in the mini-blinds. The CD player was on and Ne-Yo's "When You're Mad" floated throughout the room. I sat my bag and coat down in one of the dining room chairs, walked over to Josiah, and stood between his legs. He slid his hands into my back pockets and I placed my arms around his neck. "What's wrong?"

He shook his head.

"What? Tell me." My heart was thundering in my chest. I just knew the first word out his mouth would be about Dollah.

"I didn't get the scholarship." He twisted his lips.

"To where?" I looked at him as if I were trying to read his face.

"Syracuse."

"What happened? I thought you had it in the bag. Didn't your science grade come up? What?"

"I got a D on my report."

"D? But we outlined everything. I told you exactly what to do."

"Yeah, but I put the report together at the last minute and it wasn't as tight as it should've been. I wasn't even trippin' off it, I just figured I would get it. I never thought they would actually deny me."

"Oh . . ." I didn't mean to sound so delighted but at least Deeyah hadn't screamed on me. "Well, sweetie"—I wanted to make him feel better—"you have other colleges, right? What about Grambling? Seton Hall? Rutgers?"

"You don't understand. I wanted this. I wanted this bad."

"Well . . ."

"Well what?" he snapped. "I should've spent more time doing the report?!"

"Well, yeah . . . you should've."

He sucked his teeth. "I can't believe this." I felt like if I wasn't there he would've cried.

"It's alright, baby." I crossed my arms around the back of his neck and he began kissing me.

"You don't understand, Seven," he spoke while pulling me onto his lap. "I need you."

I knew his hands were roaming my body a little too freely, but I didn't exactly know how to say stop . . . and I didn't exactly know if I wanted him to stop, so for a moment I went with the flow. But just as I started to lose myself in how good it all felt, something screamed in my head that this was wrong . . . and all I could see was Toi saying that this is what happens when you don't listen. I felt him unbuttoning my shirt . . . and all I could think about was if I'd gone too far to tell him to stop.

He eased my zipper down and my heart raced in my chest. "You got any condoms?" I asked him, knowing that that wasn't what I meant to say.

"Yeah . . ." He started pulling my pants down. "I do."

As he went to take off my shirt I said, "Josiah, stop . . ." But I guess he didn't hear me 'cause he was beginning to feel parts of my body that I knew were taboo.

"Josiah, stop."

He still didn't stop.

"Josiah!" I screamed and pushed him off me. I quickly pulled my pants back up. "I said stop."

He leaned back and looked at me. "Here we go again."

"What you mean here we go again? I already told you what the deal was and you keep pushing."

He didn't say anything, but I could tell in his eyes he was holding a conversation with himself.

"I don't wanna disturb our flow or whatever"— I started buttoning my shirt back—"but I don't wanna do this and I'm sure of that. If you want me to leave, you know . . . I'll understand."

180

Ni-Ni Simone

"Did I ask you to leave? You runnin' again, huh? Where you runnin' to, Dollah?"

"Dollah? Is that what this is really about? What, you listening to Deeyah now?"

"At least I know she ain't lyin' to me."

"I'm not lying to you!"

"Seven, please."

"What do you mean, Seven, please?! Don't try and put this off on me! This is about you going too far and you being mad because you didn't get the scholarship you wanted. That's your fault, not mine! And yes, Dollah was my boyfriend and maybe you two don't get along but that's not my problem and I don't appreciate this!"

"Well, then maybe you oughta find something else to do, especially since you ain't doin' me."

I could swear that he heard my heart crack in half. "Excuse me, what?! What you say?"

"I'm sayin' maybe"—he shook his head—"you should step."

"Step?" *Did he really just say that? Step?*

"Yeah, bounce, like I'm gettin' real sick of playing with you. You too much work, plus you lyin' to me, and it's gettin' under my skin that you were Dollah's ex-girl anyway, especially if you were with this cat when Ibn was killed. So yeah, ma. You should bounce. I'll see you when I see you."

I did all I could to hold my tears back. I was determined he would never see me cry again. "I'm convinced that you just had a nervous break-down, talkin' to me crazy like that. But you know, my mistake for thinking you were stand-up and for thinking you were really about something. My mistake for thinking that you loved me! But you don't love me, you only love yourself! You don't deserve me, I'm too much of a diva for you. What you need is a skeezer! Stupid ass! I hate the day I ever met you! And let me just tell you this before I go, whatever hurt you feeling behind your brother, you need to get it out, because it's nobody's fault and especially not Dollah's that Ibn is dead!" I fixed my clothes, slid on my coat, and picked up my bag.

"Yo, Seven, hold up, calm down, ma, ai'ight?" Josiah stood in my way.

I shook my head no.

"You know I love you, right?" he pleaded with his eyes.

I waved my hand under my chin. "Josiah, please, it's a wrap." I took my Wifey earrings off, and threw 'em at him. "I'll hollah." And I stormed out the door.

By the time I got home, Josiah was sitting on my porch. I looked at him and couldn't feel a thing. My heart was missing, half of it was left on his floor and the other half was underneath his feet.

"Yo, let me hollah at you?" he said.

"For what," I snapped as I attempted to walk past him. "Go talk to Deeyah."

"I wanna talk to you."

"Didn't you just say you were gettin' sick of me? So be about yours and step."

"I'm being about mine and that's why I'm here."

"Don't nobody here belong to you!"

"For real, Seven, you pushin' it."

"I ain't pushing nothin'."

"Oh, okay, I tell you I love you and you just gon' play me?!"

"You don't know how to love me."

"I wanna learn."

"For what, you think it gon' get you some?"

"Get some, man, please, does that even exist with you? If I didn't love you I wouldn't be here."

"And what you want? For me to be impressed? Like for real"—I sighed—"you giving me a headache. Just disappear!"

"Oh, now I should disappear, anybody that hurts Seven should just go away? I'm not your father, I'm not about to move to California, and this ain't about to be over. But I'm not about to sweat you outside on no porch. Call me when you get your attitude in check."

"Yeah, you keep waitin' if you want to." I opened the door and slammed it in his face.

Cousin Shake was sitting on the couch in the dark with "The Best of Eric B. & Rakim" playing when I flipped on the light. "Fat Mama, what's wrong?"

Instead of telling him to mind his business I broke down and started crying. I knew I couldn't tell him the reason why, but I just needed to let it out so maybe by the morning I could let this whole thing go and my feelings for Josiah would be done and over with. "I can't talk about it, Cousin Shake."

"You can tell Cousin Shake anything."

"I just can't talk about it now."

"Okay, well you tell me when you get ready. All I want you to know is that I want what's best for you."

"Oh, Cousin Shake," I sniffed, "that was really sweet."

"Thank you, Fat Mama, because I know you want the best for me, too."

"I do."

"Well, then you need to get up off my polyester long johns. My lil' fifty-year-old tender just bought me these."

"I shoulda known it was too good to be true." I rolled my eyes and went to my room.

17

Don't break my heart
If you do I'll cry forever . . .

—SHANICE, "DON'T BREAK MY HEART"

Somebody forgot to tell me that it hurt this bad. Honestly, I didn't know I had tears like this. I go to sleep crying and I wake up in tears, because I can't stop crying. Tears are in everything I do. When I take a bath, when I'm at school, at work, at home. They're in everything and for the past three weeks that I've been crying I don't know what to do. And just when I think okay, today will be a good day, I see him staring at me in school. Or Shae gives me a note that he asked her to slide to me. Or a song plays on the radio that reminds me of how much I love him. Or I smell him, or I look too quick and swear I see him. Everything is him. It's weird, it's like my life is so mundane and so out of whack at the same time. I can't remember what I did before he was in my life. And what hurts is that every time I try to think of what I did or where I went when I wasn't with him, I come up empty, nothing comes to mind. Nothing. Absolutely nothing. And here I am, looking at a phone that doesn't ring and feeling an ache that won't go away.

It's only seven o'clock at night and already I was in bed. I held my pillow over my face and Omarion's "Ice Box" was on rotation. I don't wanna eat and I can't sleep. It's official, I'm lost and I no longer know who I am.

"Seven." Toi cracked our bedroom door open, the light from the kitchen drifting in behind her.

I didn't answer but heck, she knew I was there. She closed the door behind her and I could hear her breathing as she walked over. She was almost eight months pregnant now and her breathing started to sound like a struggling air conditioner. I wished we didn't share a room because then I could put her out.

She sat down on the edge of my bed. "Why don't you call him or talk to him?"

Tears filled my throat. "No."

"Why, Seven?"

"He didn't like me, he was using me. All he wanted to do was screw me. He wanted to come into my life, get me to love him, and then when I think that he's here and not going anywhere he tells me to step, just like Daddy did Mommy and just like Daddy did us."

"Are you listening to yourself? You're not Mommy and he's not Daddy. And Mommy and Daddy's relationship is not our problem. Stop taking that on. You have to live your life. And he loves you, Seven, he does."

"I can't talk to him. I can't." And just as I started wailing, Cousin Shake started banging on the door.

"Crying ass. 'Scuse me, I mean my dear Fat Mama, Josiah's out here. I told him I ain't appreciate you crying around here for the last year and that you ain't ate in over six months. Then I told him that you been going to bed at seven o'clock every night and that I really had a problem with him. I asked him to leave twice but he told me he wasn't here to see me. He lucky I ain't punch him in the face. I told him the next time you around here crying all night, I was gon' rock 'em to sleep."

"Yeah, Bubble Butt," Man-Man screamed. "He standing here looking at me now, and I told him you were around here passing out and carrying on, how Mommy had to have the old ladies from the church come pray over you. Just say the word and I will check this bobblehead-lookin' pop-tart right in his chin."

"Shut up!" I screamed. "Wasn't no old ladies here prayin' over me! And tell 'im I said go home."

"You tell him," Cousin Shake said. "Since you don't seem to appreciate anything me and Man-Man did and we out here helping you. We ain't the ones around here lovesick."

"Ya got that right," Man-Man said.

"Please talk to him, Seven," Toi pleaded.

I took the pillow from my face and wiped my eyes. My hair was all over the place but I didn't care, my eyes were swollen, and my gear was jacked. I wore a pair of green and white polka dot girl boxing shorts and Josiah's white tee, which still smelled like him.

When I stepped out my room, his face lit up. And unlike me he was still fine. I hated that I was still checking for him.

"You look real pretty," Josiah said.

Man-Man and Cousin Shake fell out laughing. "Well, I'll be damned," Cousin Shake said. "I done heard it all now."

"Yeah, Cousin Shake," Man-Man said, "she look like she stinks."

"That's enough!" Toi barked. "Seven, y'all should go in the living room."

When I walked in the living room my mother was coming through the door. "Josiah," she said, filled with surprise. "Hi, I'm glad to see you."

"How you doing, Mrs. McKnight?" he asked. I could hear the sadness in his voice.

"I'm fine, sweetie." My mother winked at me. "I'ma go on in here and talk to my cousin and my two other children. You two make yourselves comfortable."

Once my mother left, Josiah and I stood still and stared at each other. "So . . . wassup?" he asked.

"Nothing."

"No, real talk, keep it funky, wassup? You want

this to be over? You want me to bounce . . . for-ever?"

"Who told you that?"

"You did."

"And how is that?"

"By the way you act."

I didn't respond, instead I was silent.

"Seven," he said, "I don't even know what to say no more. I'm sorry, I am."

"You really hurt me."

"So you gon' punish me forever?"

"I just need some time."

"How much time?"

"I don't know."

"Well, yo, peep this. I'm here, but I can't keep fighting for you and you don't want me to win. So you tell me when you ready to be mine again." He reached in his jacket pocket. "I guess I assumed too fast that you would be around so I bought your ticket for you to go to my Senior's prom with me. My colors are black and silver if you're interested."

I managed to keep my I-could-care-less face on. I knew I was hurting him, but there was no way he could even begin to understand how I felt.

He placed one of the tickets in my hand. He walked toward the front door. "Just in case." He opened the door and I walked behind him. I wanted to say something to him, but I couldn't. The tears that were clouding my throat suppressed my words.

As he stepped out the door he turned around, stroked my hair to the back, and kissed me on my forehead. "Besides my mother, I've only loved two other people and they both left me." Tears filled his eyes and rolled down his cheeks. I wanted to hug him and hold him and I know I should've, but what was I supposed to say? Everybody always told me that at sixteen I was still a kid and that boys should be the last thing on my mind. That I wouldn't and didn't know what real love was, and I guess at this moment, the very moment when I should've felt grown and handled myself like the woman I needed to become, I didn't. I was a little girl and I said and did nothing. He turned away from the door and left. Now I knew for sure that I'd ran him away.

18

I got this ice box where my heart used to be . . .

—OMARION, "ICE BOX"

After Josiah left my house the other day, school wasn't the easiest place to be but I had to go. I tried not to look at Josiah as Shae and I ate lunch. "You and Melvin going to the Senior's prom?" I asked Shae.

"Girl, please." Shae smiled. "He wantin' get matchin' suits made."

"What? Gucci? And you gon' show up."

"Girl, please." Shae frowned. "I ain't hardly wearing no Gucci suit."

"Well, your man is country." I smiled for once.

"Yeah, but I ain't. I'd rather go to the prom in a boat or Cousin Shake's hearse."

"I can't wait for the Senior's prom," Deeyah said as she floated by our lunch table. "Me and Dollah gon' be beyond fly."

"Who cares?" Ki-Ki muttered as she and Yaanah walked behind Deeyah.

"I'm tellin' you." Yaanah frowned, rolling her eyes in her head. She and Ki-Ki waved as they walked by. I gave 'em half a wave but I still wasn't feeling them.

"Seven," Dollah said, sliding next to me at the lunch table. As if on cue, Josiah's eyes were glued to me.

"What?" I spat at him. "Your jump-off moving too fast for you?"

"Listen. I want you to come to the Senior's prom with me."

I looked at him like he was crazy, especially since Deeyah just passed by here and said that she was going with him. "You know what?" It was time to give homeboy the business—this had gone on long enough. "I don't know what kinda game you and homegirl are playin' but I'm not no pawn and I don't appreciate what you think you doing. I don't want you. And you know that so stop asking me stupid things and stay outta my face! I don't like you. My heart belongs to someone else and it ain't you! Now move or I swear I will slide you!"

"Oh, it's like that, Seven?"

"What"—I blinked my eyes—"you ain't know."

"I'll hollah," he said.

"Yeah, you do that." And he got up from the table and left.

As the lunch period ended, Josiah walked past

my table and nodded his head as if to say "That's right."

"Well, it's about time!" Shae said as the bell rang for us to report to class. "Now, would you please go get your man?"

19

___

"I don't believe that you had somebody make you a signature Gucci dress. You know that's not right," I said to Shae as she dressed in her Gucci tube top dress.

"Don't hate." Shae smiled. "Please don't."

She stood in front of me fully dressed. "Now give it to me."

I looked her up and down. "You fly."

"Ai'ight, girl. My man waitin' on me." She smiled, stepping into her living room where her father and a few of her aunts were snapping pictures of her and Melvin. I have to admit I was feeling some kinda way about Josiah, and although I'd worked a couple of extra hours and bought a dress, I knew there was no way he'd wanna see me. It'd been over a month since we broke up and I was sure he was over me.

Once Shae and Melvin left, I headed back home. My mother was in the kitchen cooking dinner. "Shae and Melvin look so cute."

I sat down to the table. "You saw them?"

"Yeah, when they walked out the house I was looking out the window and snapped me a picture. Shae is a part of this family, she's over here enough."

"Yeah"—I sighed—"she did look real cute."

"So"—my mother stirred a pot of rice—"you're not going, huh?"

"No," I snapped.

"You're welcome to take down that tone," my mother said, now opening a can of corn. "You know, Tina called here."

"Tina?"

"Josiah's mother."

"So what, we break up and you two become friends?"

"Umm maybe, or maybe she's just worried about her son. She called me to tell me that Josiah is going to the Senior's prom alone."

"That's nice."

"Uhmm, so you don't wanna go?"

"Nope. Sure don't."

"And why not?"

"Because Ma, all I see is Daddy when I look at Josiah and I just can't forgive him."

"Seven"—my mother turned to face me—"just like Dollah didn't kill Josiah's brother, Josiah is not your father. Stop dealing with my heartache. I know you are hurt by what your daddy did and I am, too, but you can't make Josiah pay for something he didn't do. Everybody deserves another chance."

"Would you ever give Daddy another chance?"

"If it means you living your life then maybe . . . I would."

"Do you think I know what love is, Ma?"

"I don't know, do you?"

"Yes."

"Well, then it looks to me"—she pointed at the clock—"that you better get dressed."

"Here's the dress!" Toi came rushing down the hallway.

"You were listening this whole time?" I couldn't help but laugh.

"And here are your shoes," Man-Man said.

I couldn't believe it. "Y'all set me up."

"Don't worry about that," Cousin Shake, who was dressed in his infamous MC Hammer suit, added. "Just hurry up."

"For what?"

"I'm taking you."

"Oh, no, Ma, please."

"He's taking my car, girl."

"Oh, okay." I rushed in my room and slipped on my dress, which was a gray sleeveless cocktail dress with sparkling rhinestones all over. My shoes where open toe stilettos and I had a French pedicure. Toi curled my hair in abundance of Shirley Temple curls that framed my face and complemented my deep dimples. My makeup was mostly natural and the lipstick was a shimmering MAC gloss. I have to admit I was beautiful. I just hoped Josiah thought so.

When I got to the dance I was beyond nervous. I kept holding in my stomach, somehow thinking that would help to tame the butterflies. Before I went inside, Cousin Shake kissed me on the cheek. "You look like a princess."

I was nervous and felt like I was on cloud nine when I walked into the high school gym. It was beautiful and I never would've thought that an ordinary gym could look like this. White and red balloons were everywhere, the dance floor sparkled, lights were dimmed, and the D.J. was playing Faith Evans' "Tru Love." Although I knew all eyes were on me, especially since no one expected me to come, I felt like Josiah was the only one in the place. His back was turned to me and he was leaning against the wall looking toward Shae and Melvin, who were slow dancing. I took a deep breath and walked over to him.

"It's true love," I said to him as I walked up from behind, "when you can't be without me . . . like I can't be without you."

Josiah turned around and it seemed as if his entire body lit up. He was so handsome in his black double-breasted two-piece, gray silk tie, and square toe gators. His swagger was serious and his entire look reminded me of Puffy or Jay-Z when they be throwing it on. All I could do was smile as he stared at me. "You look beautiful."

"Thank you. So do you."

"Thanks, I'm glad you came."

"I couldn't be without you."

He held me by my waist and as if on instinct, we started slow dancing. "Don't leave me, Seven."

"I'm never going to."

"You wifey, Seven."

"I'm gon' always be wifey."

"Well, I got something for you."

"What?"

He pulled my earrings out of his pocket.

"You been carrying these in your pocket?" I couldn't believe it.

"Yeah. Everyday. I've carried them everyday."

All I could do was hold him tight. "I missed you so much."

"Prove it," he said.

"How?"

"Put your earrings on."

He didn't have to ask twice. I slipped my rhinestones off and put on my bamboo heart-shaped earrings with "Wifey" on them. I know I probably looked liked Boom-Kiki from the projects, with a cocktail dress and bamboo earrings on, but at this moment I didn't care. This wasn't about nobody else but me and my boo.

20

Can't leave 'em alone . . .

—CIARA, "CAN'T LEAVE 'EM ALONE"

I woke up in the middle of the night and thought my sister was peeing on herself, until I realized it looked as if a river had exploded in her bed. "Ma!" I screamed. "Ma!" Toi's face was scrunched up in pain. "You scared?"

"Yes."

"Where is Mommy?" I fanned my face, "'cause I'm about to pass out."

"Seven," Toi panted, "I'm having contractions."

"Me, too." I started letting out short breaths. "Ma!"

"Seven, I'm having the baby, so you can calm down."

"You sure?" I think I felt my stomach cramping. "Ma!"

"WOULD YOU SHUT UP! Dang, Mommy is at work. Go wake Cousin Shake so he can take me to the hospital, call Mommy, and I need to call my doctor and Quamir."

"Quamir?"

"This is his baby," she said sternly, "and I have no time for what you think."

"Whatever!" I ran upstairs and started banging on Cousin Shake's bedroom door. As usual, he had "The Best of Run DMC" blasting. "Cousin Shake! Open up! It's an emergency! Cousin Shake!"

He snatched the door open and I immediately started throwing up. He was standing in the doorway with the biggest pair of booty-chokin' briefs I've ever seen. His stomach was hanging over the waistband and he had his hands on his hips. "Cousin Shake, Lord . . . Jesus . . . holy Ghost . . . somebody please, put some clothes on you."

"Let me tell you something, lil' girl . . ." As he spoke his belly shook. "I got a lil' shortie up in here and I don't appreciate you calling me away from my physical therapy. Now, what you want?"

"Ta-Ta-Ta-Toi is in labor."

"Good, 'bout time she got a job." And he went to close the door in my face.

"No, she's having the baby!"

"The baby?! Oh, Lord. Okay, go boil some water."

"Why?"

"I don't know. Just do it. Now let me get dressed so we can get to the hospital. Oh, and call ya mama."

I ran from Cousin Shake's room to use the phone in the kitchen. When I spoke to my mother she was calmer than I thought. All she said was to grab Toi's bag and she would meet us there.

I went back into my room, grabbed Toi's bag, and then I shut the door. Wait a minute, I forgot Toi. I am so not cut out for this. I opened the door. "I guess you need to leave with me."

"Ya think?" she snapped.

We all piled into the car. Man-Man was half-asleep but Cousin Shake was fully awake as he ran every red light in the city of Newark. "You don't know nothin' about this girl," he said. "This one of the benefits of having a tricked-out hearse—er'-body scared of you." He whipped into the hospital parking lot.

"I can see why," I said. "Cousin Shake, how are we going to get Toi out of here?"

"Better drag her ass out the back."

"Cousin Shake!" Toi screamed.

"You know I'm just playing with you, girl," he said while helping her to get out the driver's side of the car.

By the time we got in the hospital, my mother was already there. She didn't look as panicked as we did, in fact she even seemed cool. The doctors took in Toi right away and me, Cousin Shake, and Man-Man waited in the family waiting area.

After falling asleep, waking up, and pacing the waiting room floor, my mother came out and announced that Toi had a baby boy. I was so excited.

We all crept in the room, like we were scared for some reason. "Hey," I said, walking over to the bed and looking at the baby. It was hard to tell what he looked like because he was so small. Toi looked exhausted.

"How do you feel?" Cousin Shake asked her.

"Fine."

"Well, what's his name?"

"Noah."

"Noah?" Cousin Shake looked surprised. "And what's his middle name, Jesus?"

"Cousin Shake." My mother laughed. "What in the world."

"I'm just playin'—I'm just playin'."

We laughed and looked at the baby for about an hour and then my mother said we needed to leave. My sister needed her rest. I looked at Toi on the way out and I knew she was just as frightened as I felt. I never imagined she would be a mother so soon. I kissed her on the forehead and said, "I love you, big head."

"I know," she said as she drifted to sleep. "I know."

21

Ain't nothin' wrong
If you wanna do da butt all night long . . .

—E.U., "DA BUTT"

had to give it to Melvin. I had never heard of
Murfreesboro, but his dirty-dirty crew that he
imported up here had his fish fry slash birthday
party jumpin'. DC Go-Go was thumpin' and food
was everywhere. All the fish and fried cornbread
you wanted to eat or could ever imagine was making its way around the room. Even Melvin's mama
was here having her a good ole time. She was
dressed in black biking shorts, a white V-neck tee,
a red belt wrapped around her waist, some runnin' socks, and high-top L.A. Gears. She danced
over toward me and Shae and when her nephew,
Garfield, who was also the D.J., started playing
E.U.'s "Da Butt," she, along with the rest of Melvin's
down south crew, went crazy.

"Seven," Shae said as we watched everybody
get their party on. "Three o'clock." When I turned

my head to the right, it was Cousin Shake shakin' his way through the party, screaming, "This my jam right here!"

"Do it, baby!" Melvin's mother yelled at Cousin Shake.

I almost passed out. This was Cousin Shake's fifty-year-old tender? Melvin's mother? "Shake it like a salt shaker!" she said as they did "Da Butt" together. If they weren't so funny I would've been embarrassed.

"Di'ane gotta big ole butt!" the D.J. yelled.

"That's right!" Melvin's mother responded.

"Shae gotta big ole butt!"

"Oh, yeah!" Shae started dancing, which shocked the mess outta me. Not that she didn't dance, but heck, she was doing a dance that was older than she was.

"Seven gotta big ole butt."

"Oh, yeah!" Heck, if my girl could do it I figured I could do it, too. That's when Josiah walked over and whispered in my ear, "Don't make me hurt nobody in here."

And as if on cue, the music switched from E.U. to Nelly's "Flap Your Wings." All I can say is this, Cousin Shake looked to be having an epileptic seizure. This was by far the best party I'd been to in a long while.

I looked at Shae. "I gotta go to the bathroom. Hold my drink."

After a few minutes, I came back and Deeyah was all over Josiah like butter on rice, and as I contemplated if I should clown and punch her in the face or smack him, I decided to stand back and peep the situation.

Bow Wow's "Outta My System" was playing and along with Cousin Shake and Melvin's mama, who were bumpin' and grindin' and rubbin' each other, Deeyah held Josiah by the waist and swayed by herself while he stood with his arms folded across his chest, watching her carry on like she was stupid. "For real, baby," Deeyah said, "I miss you and I'm sorry. I was just trying to make you jealous with Dollah and I want you back."

"Man, please, how many times do I have to tell you I got a girl. What part don't you understand? The B or the ounce?"

"Oh, Josiah, please, you know as well as I do that big-behind Seven can't make you feel like I do."

"You know what, you can't think of nothing else to say about her but to call her a big-behind. What, you jealous 'cause she gotta better body than you? You steppin' way outta line little girl, and I suggest you play your position, which is over there to the side!"

"Oh, so you really diggin' this fat ho?!"

As Chris Brown's "Shortie Like Mine" started playing, I walked and cut in between them. Josiah placed his hands in my back pockets and I wrapped my arms around his waist. "Don't be mad 'cause this fat ho took yo' man, you thirsty trick."

"Was that nice?" He looked down into my face.

"No."

"Ai'ight then, I was handling this." He looked at

208 Deeyah as we rocked from side to side, and as if in
tune with Chris Brown he said, " 'Searched around
the world but you won't never find another shortie
like mine.'"

"Oh, no, you didn't just try and play me?! I will
turn this countrified ridiculous party out!" Deeyah
screamed. "Do you understand?! You better recognize." As she started walking toward me, Melvin's
mother stopped dancing and said to Deeyah, "We
gotta problem over here, baby? Let me know now."
She looked at me. " 'Cause Mother will handle it."

"Oh, please." Deeyah rolled her eyes. "And
what your ole country butt gon' do?" As soon as
Deeyah said that the entire party stopped and the
music literally came to a screeching halt.

"What you say now, baby?" Melvin's mother
asked, as three of the biggest women I'd ever seen
in my life gathered around her. "You didn't wanna
do nothin', now did you, baby? 'Cause we can
make it happen."

"Whatever," Deeyah snapped. "Ki-Ki, Yaanah,
let's blow this popsicle stick and beat it."

"That's what I thought," Melvin's mother said
as she snapped her fingers, and the party resumed. "They don't want nothing with Mother."

"They sure don't," Cousin Shake said. "But
Shake sure do!" And they started dancing again.

"*I said,*" Deeyah stressed, "let's go, Ki-Ki and
Yaanah."

Ni-Ni Simone

"Naw," Ki-Ki said. "I'm good. Seven"—she paused—"I'm real sorry for everything that I've done. I'm glad you and Shae made up and that you and Josiah are together, because what I did was wrong. Can you please forgive me?"

Shae pushed me on the shoulder and Josiah stared at me. "Yeah, Ki-Ki," I said reluctantly, "I accept your apology." Josiah winked his eye.

"I don't believe this," Deeyah said. "You just played yourself, Ki-Ki. Yaanah, come on."

"Girl, please." Yaanah frowned. "Seems to me you just played yourself. Why don't you get your attitude together and maybe you'll be able to keep some friends. You're just jealous of Seven and always have been. You need to get over it and stop trippin' off yourself, 'cause for real, ain't nobody even feelin' you like that."

I couldn't believe Yaanah was going off like this. For the most part, Yaanah didn't say two words. "Dang, Yaanah. Look at you!" I said.

"Girl, Seven, I been trippin' and if you'll accept my apology, I wanna become friends again."

"It's cool, Yaanah," I said. "It's cool."

"Y'all ain't even worth my time." Deeyah stormed out. "Forget y'all."

"Yo, Seven," Ki-Ki said as we all started gettin' a serious party on. "Can you introduce me to the D.J.?"

SHORTIE LIKE MINE

Ni-Ni Simone

ABOUT THIS GUIDE

The following questions are intended to
enhance your group's reading of
SHORTIE LIKE MINE.

Discussion Questions

1. In the beginning of the story do you think Josiah owed Seven an apology? Explain why or why not.

2. Do you think Seven had low self-esteem?

3. How much of Seven's belief that she was fat played in the decisions she made? If she were skinnier, do you think she would've acted differently?

4. Do you think Seven stole her friend's boyfriend? Would you ever date the same guy as your friend?

5. What did you think of Shae's life? Do you know anyone like her or her mother?

6. What lessons did you learn from the things Toi did? How different were the twins?

7. Do you think Josiah was wrong to pressure Seven to have sex with him?

8. Do you think things would have been different if Seven would've had sex with Josiah?

9. What did you think of Seven's father? Do you think he was a good father?

10. How do you think Seven's parents' marriage affected her life?

11. Do you think Seven should have forgiven Josiah sooner in their relationship?

12. Who was your favorite character? Why?

13. What character do you think you are most like?

14. What lessons did you learn from *Shortie Like Mine*?

A Discussion with the Author

What do you like most about being an author?

What I like most is that I can bring all of my dreams to life. If I want to be a singer, a dancer, or a rapper then I can be. The world on paper is limitless. But I couldn't do it without my education. And no, I'm not a walking afterschool special, but I do keep it real. I know I couldn't write books without paying attention in my English classes and when it came to the literary contracts, math was useful too—LOL.

What is one of the best things you've ever done?

Uhmmm, okay, dump a boy who didn't treat me like a lady. I had to let him know he had me twisted.

Name one of the worst things you've ever done?

Date a boy I didn't like.

Who's your favorite rapper?

You know it's Bow Wow.

Who's your favorite famous couple?

Beyoncé and Jay–Z, they are so hot!

What's your favorite TV show?

Actually I have two: *Run's House* and Keyshia Cole's reality show *The Way It Is*. Oh, and *Flavor of Love*. Wait, wait, oh yeah, BET's *Hell Date*. *I Love New York* is the bomb, too. And I do have two oldies but goodies, *Good Times* and *Little House on the Prairie*. What, chile please can you say J.J. and Nelly Olsen? I know that was more than two.

What lesson do you want readers to learn from *Shortie Like Mine*?

To never doubt yourself and to know that the sky is the limit.

Ni–Ni Simone

Stay tuned for Toi McKnight's story,
IF I WAS YOUR GIRL,
available in October 2008 wherever books are sold.
Until then, satisfy your craving
with the following excerpt.

ENJOY!

"This is my jam, right here!" I screamed as we drove down Bergen Street with the sounds of Playaz Circle's "Duffle Bag Boy" blasting from the car into the street. We'd just left the Hot 97 King Of Rap concert at the Prudential Center and were still high from the night's festivities.

"Girl, did you see how Lil' Wayne was looking at me?" my sister, Seven, said as she danced in the back seat.

"You lying, Seven," Tay laughed, as she drove down the street, looking at Seven in the rearview mirror. "You know Weezie was lookin' at me."

"I know y'all ain't on my baby daddy!" I stopped singing long enough to chime in.

"Girl, please," Seven snapped. "You got enough baby daddies!"

We all laughed as I turned up the volume and

started singing again. *"I ain't nevah ran from a damn thing and I damn sure ain't 'bout to pick today to start runnin'."*

As I threw my arms in the air, Tay said, "Toi, ain't that Quamir's truck?" She pointed across Rector Street.

I looked at the tags on the black Escalade. "Hell, yeah." I turned the music down.

"And ain't that Shanice's house?" Seven asked. "I thought he stopped messing with her."

"We don't know if that's her house," I snapped defensively. "You always jumping to conclusions."

Tay looked at me out the corner of her eyes, "You need to stop frontin'." She spat, "you know that's where the skeezer lives." Tay had double parked in the street, next to Quamir's truck. "Now the questions is, what you gon' do about it?"

"Nothin'," Seven jumped in. "You don't bring it to nobody else's spot." She sucked her teeth. "If anything we can slice his tires and bounce."

"Slice his tires?!" Tay snapped, "That is so wack." She looked at me. "You know this is ridiculous, right? And I'm not slicing no tires or breaking no windows; he gon' put up or shut up. 'Cause frankly, I can't take you crying over this dude anymore."

"Confront him and what?!" Seven spat. "If we not gon' key up his ride then we need to bounce." She turned to me, "You've seen it with your own eyes, so now you know you need to leave 'em alone." Seven wiggled her neck from side to side.

"Bounce?" Tay sucked her teeth, "girl please we 'bout to handle this."

Neither of them had noticed that I hadn't said a word. I was in shock, but then again I wasn't; I just wasn't in the mood to react to something that obviously wasn't going to change, but there was no way I could let my sister or my best friend think I was gon' allow Quamir to keep playing me. I had to stand up for something, so I twisted my neck and rolled my eyes, "I'ma ring the trick's bell."

"There it is," Tay said. "There it is, and you know I got your back."

At least for pride's sake I had to pretend like I was strong. Strong enough to at least beat this bitch's ass for being with my baby daddy. "I'm 'bout to wild out!"

"This what you do," Tay said as we got out the car. "When she comes to the door, drag her ass down the stairs. Don't even show her no mercy. She knew Quamir was your dude, yet she keeps calling him over here. Nah, we gon' end this right now." Tay's lips popped twice as she zigzagged her neck. She was the splitting image of the ghetto twins in ATL, with the attitude to match, which is why I knew that if nothing else I could always count on her to be down with the get down. Even when I just wanted to curl up and die, she was on guard.

"You know this don't make no sense, right?" Seven said as she got out the car. "Mommy will kick *our* asses if she knew we were out here like this! Forget Quamir!"

"Forget Quamir? Do you know how bad he keep doggin' this fool?!" Tay pointed at me.

"Don't call me no fool." I rolled my eyes as we walked up the steps.

"My fault." She gave me a crooked smile. "You know what I mean. Anyway, Seven, do you know this is like . . . the nineteenth time we ready to pounce on ole boy? Girl, please forget Quamir. He's takin' time away from me and my man. I wish I would—"

"Tay." I was pissed and she was making it worse. "You don't even have a man."

"Exactly," she whispered as I rang the bell. "And I'm not gon' get one chasing behind yours."

"Excuse you?" I sucked my teeth.

"Don't get mad, kick ass. Show 'em what's really hood. I'm tired of this dude playing you every other week. Shit, I need some sleep."

"This don't make no sense." Seven tapped her foot standing behind me. I could feel the warmth of her breath as she sighed against my neck.

"For real, y'all," I said. "Not now, 'cause the way I feel, y'all 'bout to get it. So my suggestion to you"—I looked at Seven and then at Tay—"is to fall back."

"Excuse you?" Seven blinked her eyes.

"Be clear," Tay spat. "T-skee ain't the one. Let Quamir and his new skeezer be the only ones you feel comfortable bringin' it to—"

"No, I don't appreciate—"

"Toi—" Tay interrupted me.

"Don't cut me off!"

"Would you shut up?!" she said tightlipped with arched eyebrows. "Somebody's comin' to the door!"

Immediately, all the air left my body as I watched Quamir open the door with Shanice standing beside him. I couldn't believe this was happening to me, especially since I knew Shanice. I mean, we weren't friends, but we went to school together and she knew Quamir was my man.

I could feel my eyes knocking in the back of my head, but now was not the time to cry. So I held my tears back as best I could, and looked at Shanice's face. I couldn't deny how pretty she was, and for a moment I wondered if Quamir thought she was prettier then me. We were both the color of fresh apple butter, yet her eyes glistened like full moons, while mine were almond shaped. I had a dimpled smile and she had a wide one. Unless I had my hair flat ironed straight—it fell over my shoulders in an abundance of ocean waves—but ole girl wore a cheap blond clip weave. Wait a minute, I just found a flaw: at least my hair is real. Now I had the souped up confidence I needed to handle my business. "This what you want, Quamir?"

"Yo," he said surprised. "What are you doing here?"

"What you think?" I pointed my hand like a gun

in his face, yet looking dead in hers. "This the tramp you want?"

"What is she doin' at my door, Quamir?! You don't be coming to my house!" Shanice screamed, jumping up and down, acting as if at any moment she was gon' bring it.

"I know she ain't stuntin'?" Tay snapped. "Oh, hell no!"

"And what?" Shanice hunched her shoulders. "He don't want her and she knows it!"

True story, I wanted to just walk away, but my mixed emotions wouldn't let me leave like that. I needed Quamir to see the pain on my face, and then maybe he would understand what he was doing to me. I felt like I was in a trance, or better yet blazed; like everything was moving in slow motion, a euphoric high that made me feel like nothing was real. Nevertheless, I had to do this. I had to teach this chick a lesson about messing with my man or better yet, teach him a lesson about messing around on me.

Therefore, I pushed all rational thought out of my mind and let my heart and bruised emotions lead the way. I reached over Quamir's shoulder and yanked Shanice by the hair. All hell broke loose! I pounced on my prey like crazy, sending the entire porch into an uproar. I'm not sure how Quamir moved out of the way, but all I knew is that he was standing there watching as I dragged her down the stairs by her hair, causing parts of her weave to fly into the breeze.

"What I tell you about my man, trick!" I swung with all I had as I pulled her into the street. The flashing streetlamp that shone above us splashed like a spotlight into her frightened face.

"Toi!" Quamir screamed, running down the stairs, the soles of his Timberlands thumping against the wood. "Yo, chill."

Chill? To hell with chill—all chill could do for me at that moment was get its ass beat.

"What?!" Tay said in killer mode. "I know you ain't tryna do nothin', Quamir!"

Quamir ignored her. Instead, he stood there watching with his left thumb tucked behind his belt buckle with a smirk on his face, all while I beat this girl down.

The girl threw a punch, but I ducked, came back up, and caught her in the chin.

"Shanice, Toi, I said chill," Quamir said with ease. I could tell he wanted to laugh because I could hear the sounds jingling in his throat.

Although Shanice was trying to fight back, I was beatin' on her like crazy as Quamir stood there and watched as if this was his favorite pastime entertainment.

"Slap her!" Tay shouted. "Her face is clear again, Toi!"

"That's enough!" Seven yelled as she tried to pull me off of Shanice. Seeing that she wasn't successful, Quamir jumped in and lifted me up by my waist. Instantly, the fight ceased.

As Quamir put me down, he stood with his

back to me as Shanice ran up and started pushing her chest against his. "Get out the way!"

My chest was heaving up and down. "Bring it!" I spat. "Bring . . . it!"

Tay shot me a high five, and wagged her tongue out like a salivating dog. "You . . . spank dat . . . ass!" She hunched her shoulders toward Shanice, who was still pushing against Quamir. "Booyah!"

"Yo'" Quamir pushed Shanice back, "What I say?!"

"Bring it! Please bring it!" I was screaming at the top of my lungs.

"Let me go, Quamir!" Shanice pushed against him and pointed at me. "I promise you, I'ma get you jumped, you ain't gon' never be able to walk these streets again! You really don't know who I am!"

"You ain't shit!" I yelled, "I just whooped yo' ass in front of your house and ain't nobody come out to help you? Girl, please."

"My mother ain't home, otherwise she'd would've shot yo' azz!"

I yawned, and tapped my lips, "what . . . eva!"

Shanice snorted, her drawstring ponytail hanging by a strand on her head. "You crazy bitch!" she struggled to reach for me, "I hate you! You know I'ma kill her, Quamir!"

"Chill," he said sternly.

"This yo' chick, Quamir?!" I mushed him in the back of his head. "This your girl?"

"I'm his baby's mother, you stupid jump-off! He told you to step but you keep holding on!"

Did she just say baby's mother? I looked at Tay for confirmation and her face went from confident and proud to surprised. Then I looked at Seven, who wore an 'I told you so' face.

Whatever. How she gon' have a baby by him and I just had one? This chick lyin'. "He ain't never told me to step," I carried on. "You wish! And girl, you don't have no baby by him. Please!" *Of all things, I know Quamir wouldn't have no baby on me. We were a family; his other two baby mamas were crazy, I wasn't, which is why he told me I was the one.* I looked at Shanice, "Lose ya'self!"

"Oh, you ain't never told her about our son, Quamir?!" Shanice said.

Son? I had the son.

"You ain't never told her to step, Quamir?" Shanice mushed Quamir in the face. "Oh, you her man?!"

"What you ain't know?!" My words floated over his shoulder. "You better tell her somethin', Quamir."

"Quamir!" Shanice screamed.

"Quamir," I shouted. "Tell her, and tell her to stop lying on you!"

Quamir's head turned back and forth from me to Shanice over and over again. For a moment, he looked as if he were going crazy, but I didn't care. I desperately wanted him to validate what I was saying and straight out call this girl a liar.

"Quamir!" Shanice and I screamed simulataneously.

"Yo, for real," he snapped. "Both y'all gettin'
on my nerves! True story, I ain't rockin' wit' neither one of y'all like that."

For some reason, as if we were doing a dance,
we all stepped back. "What you say?" I thought I'd
heard wrong.

"Oh, you ain't with me Quamir?!" Shanice spat.
"You been at my house every night this week and
we ain't together?! You're the one who asked me
to have our baby so we would be a family—"

What she just say?

"And now," she continued on, "all of a sudden
you ain't with me?!" She pushed him in his chest.
"Oh, we ain't together?!"

He asked her what . . . ?

"Go 'head, Shanice." He pointed his finger in
her face.

My voice trembled as I said, "I can't believe
this?!" I felt sooooo dumb. Here I was, battling
with a buncha lies, fighting for the sake of proving
a useless point.

"It's over, Quamir. This who you choosing?" I
pointed over his shoulder. "You can have that stank
ho! We through! You ain't nothin'; you don't take
care of your son no way. Mama's boy! Trying so
hard to be a playa but can't get outcha mama's
basement. Your whole existence is a joke. I don't
know whether to laugh in your face or spit in it."

I turned around to walk away, and Quamir
yanked me by my hair so hard that I was dizzy.
Seven and Tay immediately jumped between us. I

looked at the rage in Quamir's eyes and I knew he wasn't playing. My heart thumped in my chest. "It's cool," I said to them as they stood in front of me.

"I been waitin' to kick yo' azz!" Tay said.

"Tay!" I snapped. "Chill. Y'all move and let me hear what he got to say." Before they could move on their own, Quamir pushed them to the side and stood in front of me.

"Who you talkin' to, Toi?" he said, sounding more like my father then my man.

I didn't answer.

"Don't you ever in your stupid life talk to me like that! You so stupid and dumb. This why don't nobody else want you! And no matter how I keep tryna stay with you, you keep actin' dumb! You need to get outta my business, retarded ho! You came around here actin' like a clown and all we gon' do is laugh at you."

"Don't be talking to her like that!" Seven screamed.

"You the stupid one!" Tay said.

"I know you ain't talkin' to me, you crazyass, crackhead baby!" he spat with a sinister laugh.

"And what are you, Quamir?!" Seven said. "At least Tay got an excuse."

Tay blinked her eyes. "Excuse me?"

"Ho, please," Quamir snorted. "I'm definitely not gon' argue with no virgin."

Feeling as if I was due to pass out at any minute, I fought with all I had to at least sound strong.

"Boy, please. you been with this raggedy ho all week, and you talkin'!" The tears dancing in my throat stopped me midsentence. "This really yo' baby mama, Quamir?"

"Did I tell you I had another baby? Uh, answer me!"

Silence.

"Answer me!" he screamed.

"No!"

"Well then, why you assuming things?"

"What?!" Shanice screamed, a flood of tears streaming down her face. "So what is you sayin'? That we don't have a son?!" She punched him in his chest. "You sayin' he ain't yours?"

"Stupid tramp!" I tossed in the wind. "This broad really got a baby by you?" Suddenly, I felt like my son had been reduced to nothing. He wasn't the oldest, he wasn't the youngest, he wasn't even the one by the baby mama his daddy loved. He was just one of Quamir's kids. "You ain't nothing Quamir! Matter of fact, it doesn't even matter what you do 'cause I'm out!"

"And I'm done with you, too," Shanice said. "I'm sick of you cheating on me!"

"Hos is always schemin'," Quamir said. "Man, please. Both y'all knew the deal and now you tryna act like you ain't know about the other? Now if you wanna stomp each other, then don't talk about it, be about it!" He stepped from in front of me. "What I care!"

Shanice started going off on Quamir, but I

stood there. Stunned. Embarrassed. Wishing I could fly away and nobody would see me. Although he hadn't hit me, I felt like I'd been beaten. Why would he play me like this? What happened to him falling on his knees and telling this chick I was wifey?

I became anxious and didn't know what to do, where to turn, or how to act. I thought about crying but couldn't get any tears to come out. Then I thought about dying, but thinking of my son reminded me I had a reason to live. Then it hit me: I felt like nothing, as if all my wind had been sucked out and all that was left was a worthless shell.

"I'm leaving," Seven spat. "If you wanna stay here and take this crap, then do you. But me, I'm outta here!"

I stood there for a moment before walking backward to the car and getting in. I knew I looked crazy; I felt out of my mind. As the three of us got in the car and slammed the doors, I tried my best to believe what I was about to say. "I am so done with his ass!" I sniffed as tears covered my cheeks like glaze. "And I know he gon' come back beggin' me . . . like he always does. But I promise you, he gon' have to work real hard to get back with me. 'Cause I'm not beat for this no more!"

"You sound," Seven said, shaking her head as we drove off, "so damn dumb."